Montana Cowboy Miracle

MONTANA COWBOY MIRACLE

A Wyatt Brothers Romance

JANE PORTER

TULE
PUBLISHING

DEDICATION

For all those who need to be seen and heard.
I see you, I hear you.
You matter, immensely.

ACKNOWLEDGEMENTS

Thank you to all of you who always have my back. You know who you are. I'm so very grateful, especially this year with all the changes.

Thank you to the incredible team at Tule for your support while I write, and then the care you put into my books after: Cyndi, Meghan, Nikki, Monti, and Marlene—thank you! You all work so hard to make me look good.

Thank you Lee for always giving me such beautiful covers…eight years of them!

Thank you, Barbara Ankrum for your editing on this one. It needed you and you were the perfect person to bring out the best in Cade and MerriBee.

Thank you Lee and Janine for your social media expertise. Thank you Denise for all your assistance with film. Thank you to my Street Team, you don't just support my books, you support me, and are true friends. I love each of you!

Thank you to my family for letting me feed you far more take out than you'd like during the last few weeks of my deadline. Thank you to my Ty for being my hero, my husband, my best friend. You changed the way I look at life, and the way I love.

Dear Reader,

MONTANA COWBOY MIRACLE is book four in my six book Wyatt Brothers of Montana series, and I've enjoyed writing this series so much. The Wyatts are a close family, but the hero in this story, Cade Hunt, has never had what the Wyatts have: stability, security, unconditional love. He's looking for his past to find answers, and that search leads him to Marietta and Paradise Valley. It also takes him to Merri Bradley's "Christmas House" which is the last place he wants to be.

MerriBee isn't interested in romance. She isn't focused on family, children or love. In fact, she's so busy taking care of others that she doesn't even realize she has any wants or needs. It's not until tough rancher Cade Hunt arrives on her doorstep that she begins to discover just how much she is missing in life.

Sometimes we have to change, and make sacrifices, in order to grow. Sometimes we have to let go of one dream, to discover another. Cade and MerriBee definitely have their challenges, but they preserve and get their happy-ever-after. (Thank goodness!)

Ever since I finished writing MONTANA COWBOY MIRACLE, I've been waiting for Christmas. I love Christmas—not the hustle bustle, or the shopping—but the beautiful lights, the warmth, the hope, the sacredness of the season. I am a woman of faith, and my hope is that my story will lift you, give you joy, and remind you how much you matter, because you do.

Merry Christmas,
Jane

PROLOGUE

THREE TIMES A week Cade Hunt had dinner with his boss, Dorothy Warner, in the dining room of the sprawling log cabin built early in the 1920s when the US National Parks were constructing their great lodges. The big Wyoming house echoed the influences of Park Architecture. The dining room's rustic beams were stenciled in pale gold, the fabric on the oversized chairs a rich blue with a Native American motif, and the huge leaded windows overlooked a garden that was now dormant and covered in snow.

Cade was the only Sundowner Ranch employee who regularly took meals with Dorothy, or Dot, as he called her. Sometimes Emma, the big house cook and housekeeper, would join her for a bite, maybe dessert. But that was a rare occasion. Then they'd sit in the family room and watch *Jeopardy!* and enjoy the homemade cake or pie that Emma had made that day.

Cade and Dot were close and had been since he was a rebellious teenager looking for a place to land since home had been anything but easy. Dot had never married or had children, and had a reputation for being tough, but she'd taken a liking to Cade, and had stuck her neck out for him on more than one occasion, pushing him to learn, and grow. To be a better man.

It was Dot who preached forgiveness, something that wasn't his strength. She also recommended forgetting, something else he didn't do well. But he tried, for her sake.

There weren't many people Cade cared about, but Dot was one. The number one. And then there was his missing sister, and if he ever found her, he wouldn't let her go.

"Don't be angry, Cade," Dot continued, folding her crimson cloth napkin and placing it next to her plate on the table, her thin hand trembling ever so slightly. "This isn't a punishment. I'm not singling you out—"

"But you are," he interrupted. "I'm the only one you're telling to get lost this Christmas."

"I'm not telling you to get *lost*. I'm telling you that this is a good time to go look for your sister. You say you want to find her, but you keep putting it off."

"Because I've run out of leads."

"What about your father? Then find him."

"That's different. He could have found me—"

"Not if he didn't know about you." Dot lightly drummed her fingertips on the table. "You should give him a chance. Find out the facts. You've always wanted to know the truth. Here's your chance."

"I'll reach out after the holidays."

"I'll need you after the holidays. Go now. Take some vacation. Enjoy Montana."

"I'd rather be here. This is my home. Unless you're firing me."

She rolled her eyes. "You know I'd never do that. You're indispensable. I can't imagine the Sundowner Ranch without you on it."

Cade folded his arms over his chest. "So why ask me to take off until after Christmas?"

"You need a vacation. You never take one."

"I don't."

Dot's tone grew as flinty as his. "Fine. Let's put the cards on the table, Cade. Alistair and his family have asked that you give them space this year. But you won't if you're here. You'll be you, which is what *I* like, but it's what they don't like. You're intimidating."

He made a rough sound of disgust. "I'm not."

She smiled faintly, expression warm, amused. "Not to me. But my family—"

"Are useless."

"Your animosity puts me squarely in the middle."

"It's difficult to watch them push you around. They talk down to you. They act like the ranch is already theirs. I can't leave you alone here."

"I'm old, not feebleminded. And for the good or the bad, they are my family. I can handle them."

"They'll run you ragged, Dot. They did last year. You had pneumonia after they left, were sick for weeks." He didn't add that it was touch and go for a bit, with even the doctor wanting to hospitalize Dot. Instead, they got her an oxygen tank for home, but Cade and Emma rarely left her side.

"I won't push myself so hard this year. I acknowledge my limits."

"But *they'll* push you hard. Without me here, they'll walk all over you, and I won't allow it. I won't permit—"

"This, Cade, is what Alistair objects to," she interrupted. "You're half my nephew's age, but you act like the boss."

"I am the boss." He saw her arch an imperious eyebrow. "You pay me to be the boss."

"I pay you to manage the ranch, not them. Or me." She eyed him for a long moment, her small turquoise and silver earring catching the light. "You're taking this so hard, my dear. You should be delighted to have some time away, time to yourself."

"I prefer being here with you," he said stubbornly.

She reached out, patted his arm. "I know. And I like you here. But Alistair is having panic attacks, or whatever they're called, anticipating more conflict with you. He says he can't be manhandled this year."

"I've never laid a hand on him."

"Apparently you glower." Dot's lips twitched. Her eyes shone with humor. "You make him uncomfortable."

"Good."

"It's only for three weeks and a bit. A change will be

good for you. You haven't been away in years. Go travel, see the world, enjoy yourself, if you won't look for your sister." When Cade's mouth opened, she cut the protest off quickly by adding firmly, "It's not a request, Cade. It's an order. Boss to employee, you've earned months of vacation time, use some of it."

He couldn't speak for a moment. She'd never made him leave before, for anyone, or anything. "When do I go?"

"They begin arriving Thursday night. So, Thursday morning?"

"You don't have the tree up. Nothing's decorated yet."

"You hate everything to do with Christmas. You should be relieved."

"But I always help you—"

"And this year they will help me." She gave him a serene smile, a smile that indicated they were pretty much done.

He wasn't ready to let it go, though. Nor was he ready to be sent off for the next three weeks. "This is a bad idea, Dot."

She just gave him that smile again. "We'll see."

He didn't exactly stomp out of the room, because he wasn't eleven, and he wasn't having a tantrum, but he didn't leave in a good mood, nor give her that gentle pat on her shoulder as he left. Returning to his bunkhouse, a log cabin that had been the original Warner homestead, a cabin that had been his ever since he'd taken over as ranch manager four years ago, he shut the door harder than necessary. The logs in the cabin were stained dark, but the cabin was sturdy despite its age. Thanks to fresh chinking, and a new wood shingle roof, it was warm, dry, and homey. Usually, Cade took comfort in the snug log cabin, but tonight he tossed his coat off, tugged off his boots and threw himself down on the long leather couch fronting the fireplace.

He was *not* on board with Dot's plan. There was nothing about her plan that he liked, but seeing as he worked for her, it wasn't as if he could push back too hard.

And yet, if her family was coming in, he wanted to keep an eye on her. Make sure she wasn't being overly taxed, or harassed. Last year the Jameses hounded her their entire visit, wanting to know her future plans, wanting to know what provisions she had made for them in her will. For heaven's sake—who asked an elderly family member about their will?

Who had the audacity to do such a thing?

He wouldn't call her relatives gold diggers, but they certainly weren't visiting her every Christmas because they enjoyed her company. No, in their minds, Great-Aunt Dorothy represented financial security. She was their lifeline. But what had they ever done for her? When had even one of them cared about her as a person?

Cade had known Dot since he was sixteen—over half his life now. Her family had never even shown up until a few years back, when out of the blue, they decided it was time they all started spending the holidays together, which meant that Dot hosted them all. And every year like clockwork now, they flew in from wherever they lived, expecting rides to and from the airport, as if the ranch hands were chauffeurs. Cade had never once complained as he ferried them back and forth, and he had never objected to their endless requests, usually impatiently delivered as if Dot's old rambling house, was a five-star resort, staffed for their pleasure. No, he didn't ever protest—although he'd refused the folded five- and ten-dollar-bill tips because that was just too much—but on the inside, he seethed because as they swanned around the old house, speaking of Dot as if she were a child, someone who didn't know her own mind, someone who couldn't be trusted to run the ranch now that she was *old*.

But Dot, at ninety-two, was sharper than the rest of the Jameses put together. She'd grown up on this ranch, a ranch founded by her grandfather. She'd had three brothers, two died during the World War, and the other had been killed in a car accident his sophomore year at Yale. As a teenager, she became her father's right hand. Even today she rode during the roundups. She oversaw the branding. She personally read every contract and agreement. Yes, she'd ask Cade's opinion, but it was most definitely her ranch.

Her family, these nieces and nephews, and great nieces and nephews—didn't know the first thing about the Sundowner Ranch and every year after arriving they'd poke into closets, examine paintings, discuss the value of the artwork and carpets, the furniture and books. Dot wasn't even dead and they were putting a price on everything, divvying it up among themselves.

And now they'd found a way to get rid of him.

Cade wasn't happy at all.

CHAPTER ONE

THE SNOW WAS falling, the small town silent and still beneath the blanket of white. Merri Bradley, or Merri-Bee as her friends and patients called her, left the hospital, driving with care as she exited the hospital parking lot, and then bumped over the railroad tracks.

It was a quiet morning, snow softly tumbling from the sky, no traffic on the roads. Downtown remained dark, most businesses still closed, although the Java Café was open, and warm yellow light glowed from the big glass windows of Main Street Diner.

MerriBee parked on Main Street, taking one of the empty spaces in front of the diner and stepped from her car. Her right foot did a slide on a patch of ice, and she caught the side of her Subaru, steadied herself, before heading inside. The diner was warm, and smelled of bacon, coffee and cinnamon—three of her favorite scents. She took her coat off just inside the door, hung it on the rack provided, and swiped a hand over her head, brushing off snowflakes, even as she took her favorite chair at the long counter.

Flo stopped in front of her to pour a cup of steaming

coffee. "Ready to order, hon? Or do you want a few minutes?"

Flo had been at the diner ever since MerriBee arrived in town. Apparently, she was a Marietta institution, much like the courthouse, or Grey's Saloon. MerriBee shook her head. "Think I'll just sit with coffee for a little bit. Need to unwind."

The older waitress's forehead creased. "Long night?"

MerriBee fought the ache in her chest. "A very long night."

"You do a job most of us couldn't do. Don't know how you have the strength. I could hardly handle my mom's passing, not sure how you do it over and over."

MerriBee managed a faint smile even though her eyes burned. Her heart hurt right now, but then, it always did when it came to the goodbyes. "Well, I couldn't be on my feet, serving people all day," she said, forcing a note of cheer into her voice. "We all have a different calling."

"Yes, but helping folks die isn't the easiest of callings."

Again, MerriBee struggled against the weight in her chest, pressing down, making it hard to breathe. Death was never easy, not even when it was a relief. "You make it feel like I'm in the business of euthanasia. It's hospice work."

"A death doula," Flo said. "Isn't that what you called it?"

"I do both. I'm a hospice nurse and yes, when needed, a death doula." Her expression shifted, her mouth quivering. It had been such a long night. So difficult. Sometimes people were ready to go, and sometimes they weren't. Last night was one of those nights where her patient wasn't ready. Those deaths were the hardest of all.

MerriBee reached up to slide a fingertip beneath her eye, and then the other, drying the tears before they could fall. "Ignore me. I'm not in the best form. I'm going to eat something in a bit and—"

"Go home and get some sleep, I hope."

"Exactly what I intend to do."

"Good. You look tuckered. So, when you're ready, just let me know and I'll get your order in."

"Thanks, Flo." MerriBee watched her move on to other diner customers, pouring coffee, clearing plates, chatting away. So like Flo, so like the diner. When MerriBee had moved to Marietta eight years ago, she'd felt like an outsider. But over the years, Marietta had become home, and the people in this town had become her people, her friends as well as her family, as she didn't see her own family very often anymore.

There never had been a big falling out with her family; they all had just... grown apart. Her career didn't help. Her parents couldn't relate to her job, and she couldn't understand why they were so happy with their structured routine. It was always the same. Spaghetti on Monday, chicken on Tuesday, some kind of casserole on Wednesday, meat loaf on Thursday, and so forth. The menu never changed. The TV shows rarely changed. News was always watched, local news at five, national news at six. Dinner was scheduled around the news, too, with her mother serving everything promptly at 6:45.

It wasn't the worst way to live, but it wasn't MerriBee's vision for her future. No, she wanted bigger things for herself. Her parents were baffled by her as a girl, but they loved her, and she loved them, and if she needed a parent fix, they weren't that far, just over the mountains in Spokane, Washington. Her parents had only come once to see her in her eight years in Marietta, which was a shame as she had plenty of space in her house. Admittedly it was a very big house for one person, and she'd bought it as a single woman, following the death of John. It was why she'd begun renting out rooms, usually to families of patients she cared for. She'd never intended to rent out rooms, but the income was welcome, and it made her old Queen Anne house, built during the turn-of-the-century, feel like a home. As well as making her feel needed.

No one had understood why she'd buy such a big house—a rather dilapidated house—after she was widowed. But houses in good neighborhoods held their value, and she trusted real estate more than the stock market. She also couldn't stay in her old home, the one she'd been living in during her brief marriage as that was where John died, and it was too painful staying there.

John. She exhaled softly, just as she did whenever she thought of him. It was five years ago this month since he died. Time was strange. Sometimes it seemed so slow, but looking back, it amazed her that five years had passed since his death.

She'd known from the moment she met him, he wouldn't be with her long, but that hadn't stopped her from falling in love with him. Maybe she'd loved him so intensely because she knew their time was limited. Or maybe it was just John. He was everything she'd ever wanted in a partner, everything she admired in a man. But he had bone cancer and it was ravaging him, and there was little medicine could do anymore.

It was falling in love with John that shifted her from the neonatal unit to hospice. There were a lot of nurses able and willing to take care of the preemies, but fewer interested in hospice. But just because she could do it, didn't mean it was easy. It was never easy. Every death was hard. Every loss made her heart hurt. And losing Missy this morning had been particularly brutal. She'd been such a fighter, all the way to the end.

Even at the end.

MerriBee's phone rang. She considered not answering, but she saw it was Finn from the Bramble House, the historic red brick B&B a block down Bramble Lane from her house. "Hi, Finn," she said, taking the call. "How are you?"

"I'm good. Hopefully I'm not interrupting anything."

"I've wrapped up my shift. I'm just at the diner, waiting for breakfast. What can I do for you?"

"I'm in a bind and was wondering if you have any rooms available for the week. We don't overbook often, but we did this week. Do you have space for one guest? Cade Hunt runs Sundowner Ranch in the Big Horn Mountains. We vacationed there a year ago, did the whole dude ranch experience with the kids. He's a very nice man and I hate to send him to the Graff. It's not his kind of place."

"Is he that picky?"

"It's just the opposite. He likes quiet places, without a lot of fuss. You know how busy the Graff gets this time of year. And hopefully it'd only be for a week. I'm trying to move some things around so he could be here the second week."

MerriBee had a problem saying no to people. She had a feeling others knew that about her, too. "He's in town for two weeks?"

"He has some business with the local ranchers. I don't see him sitting around your house all day."

MerriBee hesitated, and then thought of the income, because income was always nice, particularly with the giving she did this month. "Okay. Send him my way."

"I'll call and give him your address. I imagine he'll be there around noon."

"And his name is Hunt?"

"Yes, Cade Hunt. Thanks, MerriBee, much appreciated."

MerriBee hung up and looked down at her paper place mat and the water glass leaving a damp ring. It was just a week. She could handle a week. As long as he didn't expect too much company or hand holding since she was ready for a break. It was time for a break. Finally.

Flo returned. "Reading to put in that order?"

MerriBee managed a tired smile. "The usual."

"I thought so."

Five minutes later, a plate of scrambled eggs arrived, with a small serving of corned beef hash and one slice of wheat toast lightly buttered. She forced herself to eat, knowing she'd feel better if she did. Her last meal had been… what… almost twenty hours ago? Twenty-four? It was good she was now officially on holiday. Every year since John died, she took the month of December off. It was her time to rewind, reset, and take care of herself.

And put together her Christmas baskets, but she wouldn't think about those today. They weren't being delivered for two and a half weeks and she had everything organized.

MerriBee left money on the counter, tucked beneath her plate. Flo never gave her a bill. No one at the diner did. It made her a little bit crazy. She wasn't charity, nor was she poor, and so always left a generous tip. The tip was her way of saying thank you. Thank you for the love. Thank you for the support. The community had been there for her when John died. They were still supportive. She was lucky to have found Marietta, lucky to have work and a meaningful life.

The snow was still falling as she drove home. There were more cars out now, more lights on in homes. Some folks had their Christmas lights still on. In other homes, she could see a glimpse of glowing Christmas trees. Most of the houses on Bramble Lane had wreaths, and greenery somewhere. Bramble was admittedly the nicest street in Marietta, at least in historic Marietta. There were plenty of huge homes in Paradise Valley, and new big homes being built on the outskirts of town, but Bramble Lane was lined with charming Victorian and Queen Anne homes, homes built during the heyday of the copper rush. Her home was by no means as big as Bramble House itself, or the others down by the park, but it was two stories, with big bay windows, dark red paint, and wide, crisp white trim.

Years ago, the children on the street nicknamed her house the Christmas House because of the color scheme, and it had stuck. It didn't hurt that she loved to decorate the house for the holidays. Festive and fun were the keywords. Every December her beautiful house became her own private escape.

Pulling in front of her house, she carefully turned into her narrow driveway, and as she turned off the engine, she drew a deep breath then exhaled, letting some of her tension go. It was her routine every time she returned home from caregiving. Slow deep breath. Hold it in, then slow steady exhale. Release the hurt, release the grief, find the joy, find the hope. Life was a gift. You just had to appreciate it.

As she walked up to her porch, shoes crunching frost on her sidewalk, she smiled at the wreath with angels on the front door. She already felt better. Just being home was good. Now all she had to do was get Mr. Hunt's room ready, and then she could take a much-needed nap.

CADE HUNT PULLED up to this two-story house that looked like a gingerbread house with its white trim and charming front porch. He shifted into park, temper stirring. He'd only found out a few hours ago that Bramble House had made a mistake in their booking, and had shifted his reservation to the Christmas House.

This wasn't where he wanted to stay. He didn't do festive and the house was irritatingly cheerful with the fresh white snow on the roof like thick icing, the exterior a warm barn red, the two-story house framed by tall evergreens, the layered branches dusted white as well.

Just a few days, he told himself. It would only be temporary and then he'd be back at Bramble House. Eliza had assured him she'd be able to work him in early next week, and he trusted her.

Cade turned off the engine, stepped from his truck, and grabbed his duffel bag from the backseat of the cab. The sidewalk was lined with three-foot plastic candy canes. The dark green door shouted Christmas with a huge wreath with red and white checked bows and fabric gingerbread boys and girls. Child-sized nutcrackers in a glossy red and blue flanked the door. He touched one. It was painted wood. Dot would be laughing if she saw him here. He'd never comment on her holiday decorations again.

He rapped firmly on the green front door and waited. The house was quiet. He continued to wait another moment and knocked even more firmly. Still nothing. His mood went from bad to worse. Eliza had assured him he was expected.

Cade leaned on the doorbell, giving it an extra-long push. If that didn't work, he was gone—

The door swung open, and a young woman stood in the doorway, her face flushed, a crease on one pink cheek. "Mr. Hunt?" She greeted him breathlessly.

She was pretty, ridiculously pretty, high cheekbones, beautiful eyes, a full soft mouth. Her hair—long red curls—fell loose over her shoulders. If she was wearing makeup, he couldn't see any, and yet her black eyelashes framed eyes so intensely blue green they reminded him of the turquoise jewelry Dot liked to wear.

"Yes, ma'am," he answered, guessing her age to be mid to late twenties. He couldn't imagine her any older than that.

"Mrs. Bradley is fine," she said with a warm smile. "Or better yet, just call me MerriBee. Everyone else does. Did you have any difficulty finding the house?"

Mrs. Bradley? She was married then? But of course she was. She was stunning, and she had a smile that probably broke a lot of hearts.

"No problem," he answered. "Very easy to find."

"Good. Sometimes it it's hard after it snows." Her small, straight nose wrinkled. "But then you're from Wyoming. You're comfortable with snow."

"I am," he answered. "How did you know I was from Wyoming?"

"Eliza mentioned you run a dude ranch in the Big Horn Mountains."

"It's a proper ranch, but yes, in summer, they open it to families who want to play cowboy."

The edge of her lips curled. "You don't approve?"

"It's not my ranch."

She arched a brow but said nothing else. Instead, she gestured for him to enter. "Do you have anything else?" she asked, just before closing the door.

"This is everything."

"Okay." She shut the door, flicked on some light switches. "Let me show you around."

She led him down the hallway pointing out things on her way. "Kitchen is to the left. I'll show you that better later, but it's always open, always yours. Treat it like your kitchen—" She flashed him a quick smile. "Hopefully, you keep your kitchen clean. I'm happy doing my own dishes, but—"

"Don't worry. I know how to clean up after myself."

"I hope I didn't offend you, just thought we'd establish ground rules upfront."

"It'd take a lot more to offend me." His gaze stopped, resting on the decorations everywhere. This was undoubtedly the most festive house he'd ever seen. Wreaths, garland, lights, Santas, nativity sets, Christmas trees. Red, green, and white. Personally, it was a lot, but it wasn't his house. And he had his own room. It wasn't as if he had to spend all his time in the living and dining room. "Any other rules I should know?"

"Not really rules, I wouldn't put it quite that way. Just things that make it more comfortable for you and me sharing space over the next few days." She smiled brightly. "But yes, little things like, if something runs out, or we need some more of something, if you could just add it to the shopping list I keep on the counter in the kitchen, that'd be great. I generally keep all the doors locked, but you'll have your own key. Lots of people in Marietta don't lock their doors, but I do, just because."

"That's easy enough."

"I like to leave the outside Christmas lights on until eleven each night. They're all on timers and go off then. The Christmas tree in the living room is on a timer as well. So, you don't need to ever worry about turning any of them off, as that's handled."

"Again, good to know."

"I'm happy to pick up groceries for you if you make the list, or for something special you want to drink in the morning. I have coffee, tea, hot chocolate—" She broke off and looked at him expectantly.

"I just drink black coffee. Keep it simple."

"I always have plenty. And if you want a different kind—"

"Not picky. Just drink it strong."

"Perfect." She continued down the hall, pointing to rooms. "You've seen the living room, and dining room. There's a study on that side, overlooking the street, and then a guest room, downstairs here at the end for those who need a more accessible friendly room and bathroom. When no one is here, I use it for a craft room."

At the end of the narrow hall was a second stairwell, paneled in a warm, rich wood. It was narrow but elegant with a gleaming bannister. "I frequently use these stairs to the second floor as it's shorter when I'm going from my bedroom to the craft room." She led the way up, turning on more lights. "On the second floor there are four rooms. My bedroom, two guest rooms, and a small sitting room, which was once a sewing room. It gets lovely morning light and many of my guests enjoy a cup of tea or an afternoon glass of wine there, as in summer you see the most gorgeous sunsets."

"That's my room," she added hastily, pointing to a closed door nearest the narrow stairs they'd just climbed. "Yours is there, but if you prefer the bear room over the train room, you can switch."

"You've named your rooms?"

"They're just the themes." Pink suffused her cheeks. "You have a key to your bedroom, and once you're settled, I won't be going in, unless it's laundry day, and I'm changing the sheets—"

"I can change my own sheets."

"It's part of the service—"

"I can do my own laundry, and change my sheets," he repeated.

"Very well. I won't be going in your room at all then."

"I won't be going in your room either," he said, respecting her for covering the house rules.

"Well," she said, returning to his door and handing him the key. "I should probably just leave you to settle in."

Alone in his room, Cade couldn't mask his horror.

This wasn't just a house decorated for the holidays, but it literally was a *Christma*s house. Everything was red and green... every surface looked festive. It was as if a Christmas bomb exploded, covering walls, floors, windows with ribbons and bows and glitter. He didn't even know if it was tastefully done. It was just done, and it hurt his eyes. He didn't do Christmas, and he certainly didn't want, or need, a Christmas tree in his bedroom. Or a train that went around the upper walls on a track that hung just beneath the thick creamy-white crown molding.

He reached for his phone to call Eliza at Bramble House. Surely there had to be someplace else he could stay.

MERRIBEE RETURNED DOWNSTAIRS and went to the kitchen to make tea. She felt the need of something warm, her insides wobbly.

He reminded her of John. But she wasn't sure why. Cade Hunt was certainly bigger, taller, with a much more muscular build. She wasn't sure if it was his facial features, or the color of his eyes, but there was something in his face, something about him that made her think of John and it was both good and bad, because she hadn't felt that ache in her chest for a long time. She hadn't grieved for him for a while now. Was that a bad thing?

MerriBee knew John was the last person who would want her still grieving, five years after his death, and yet she balked at letting him go. Still. If she didn't remember him, who would?

So many people didn't understand why she hadn't married again, but the first few years after his death were incredibly difficult, and then by the time she thought she might be ready to meet someone, she realized she felt too old, too out of step with most men her age. She'd been through so much in such a short period of time, it had aged her, and changed her, and she didn't regret it. Not at all. But trying to find someone who could relate to her—odd girl that she was—seemed incredibly unlikely and finding someone she could love after John... well, that would take a miracle.

Even if her marriage had only lasted eleven months, with most of it spent in a hospital.

MerriBee heard footsteps on the stairs and she quickly straightened, blinking, trying to pull herself back to the present. What was she doing in the kitchen? Why had she come here?

Ah, tea. Right.

She filled the kettle, turned on the gas burner, and stood there, next to the stove, waiting for the water to boil.

Waiting for Mr. Hunt to appear.

And then he did.

He was still wearing his heavy sheepskin coat and carrying his hat and duffel.

There was something in his expression that made her heart do an uncomfortable thump. "You're leaving," she said, voice quiet.

"I don't think this is the best fit for me," he said, his blue gaze meeting hers. His expression wasn't unkind, but his gaze was direct. "And I mean you no offense, Mrs. Bradley."

"What's wrong?"

"It's just a lot of… merry and jolly."

He might have reminded her of John, but he wasn't John. "And you don't like merry and jolly."

His square jaw eased, his lips softened slightly. "I'm sorry."

"Where are you going to go?"

"There's another bed-and-breakfast a couple blocks from here. They had space."

"You called around?"

"Eliza did."

She swallowed hard, hurt, but not even sure why she

should feel rejected. She didn't know him. What he thought of her—and her house—shouldn't matter.

But for some unfathomable reason, it did.

IT WAS JUST a short drive to the B&B, literally down the street, and Cade's welcome was brisk and professional, polite without being overly friendly. There was a humble wreath on the front door, and a modest Christmas tree in the corner of the living room, but that was pretty much it for holiday décor. Thank goodness.

Cade settled into his room—this time on the ground floor—with the navy and cream paisley comforter cover and matching pillow shams. The curtains were navy. The towels were beige. The bed was firm. The dresser probably an antique. His kind of room. Simple and practical.

Yet he felt guilty for leaving the Christmas House. In hindsight, it struck him as a petty, mean-spirited thing to do, especially as MerriBee Bradley seemed like a nice person, as well as a *beautiful woman*, a small voice inside his head added, but that was neither here nor there. He'd left, settled here, allowing him to focus on why he was in Marietta—to find his family, and not be distracted by Christmas or stunning redheads. Cade's first crush was a redhead. Sinead Halligan had copper-colored hair and wore it in two long braids. She had freckles as well, mostly on her nose and cheeks, and he liked those, too. He touched them once and got in trouble, sent to the principal's office where he had to explain to the principal he wasn't being rude, that he thought they were pretty.

He never kissed Sinead, although he'd wanted to, but if he got in trouble for touching her cheek, he certainly wasn't going to kiss her lips.

He didn't kiss a redhead until seventh grade. Her name was Shelley and her hair was dark red, and she didn't have freckles, just pale skin that looked perfect, almost translucent. He kissed her at a birthday party, during a game of seven minutes in heaven. The seven minutes wasn't enough for him. They ended up going steady until her dad found out and told her that Cade wasn't good enough for her. Cade didn't dispute it. He wasn't a good student. He didn't come from one of the nice families. But he had something others didn't—he had confidence. And maybe it wasn't much, not compared to money, or class, but it helped him get by.

There were no more redheads until he was sixteen, and he was working his first summer at the Sundowner Ranch. Tara Huntley was British and the daughter of a very wealthy man—her dad was a lord or something back in England— and Cade fell for her accent, her long strawberry-blonde hair, and the way she looked in her jeans. She didn't have time for him, and did her best to ignore him, apparently was way too good for him, until her last night at the ranch, when Tara seduced him.

One of the other summer ranch hands reported him, and

the next morning after the Huntleys departed, Cade was called before the ranch manager. The ranch manager said a lot of unpleasant things before telling Cade to pack up and clear out. Cade was in the middle of packing when Miss Dorothy Warner, owner of the Sundowner Ranch, appeared in his bunkhouse wearing her custom white western blouse, jeans, and boots. She asked him a few questions, and he answered truthfully—it was his first time breaking rules, he understood it was wrong, he had no excuses, he was sorry, too.

Miss Warner to him then, just looked at him for a long minute. "I have a feeling about you," she said at length. "You've got something in you. I believe in you."

It was the first time anyone had said anything like that to Cade. *I believe in you.* No one believed in him. No one saw anything good in him, but she did. This fine woman who owned, and ran, one of the biggest ranches in Wyoming. He almost cried. He teared up, and his throat swelled close.

"I'll give you one more chance," she said. "Stay away from the guests. I don't care how pretty, or how flirtatious, but there's no fraternizing with the guests. It's your job to protect them, not make love to them."

He flushed with shame, and he stared at the ground, wanting to disappear.

"You know the rules here."

Cade nodded.

"Bob wants you gone," she added. "But I'm giving you one more chance. Give me your word that you'll respect the rules and honor the Sundowner code of conduct."

"What's that, ma'am?"

"You don't know it?"

He looked up at her, gave his head a slight shake.

"It's how my daddy was raised, and how he raised my brothers and me. It's how I live my life and I now expect it of you." Her brown eyes locked with his. "Are you listening?"

"Yes, ma'am."

"Cowboys have integrity. Cowboys don't lie, cheat, steal, or bring dishonor on themselves, or their ranch. You use your head, listen to your heart, and respect those around you. You take care of all animals. You protect people. And you only fight if that is your very last option. Understand?"

"Yes, ma'am."

"I'm not going to bail you out of trouble again, but if you need help, real help, I'm here for you. But I can't play favorites, so it's time you earned your place here." She stuck out her hand. "Deal?"

He shook her hand. "Deal."

And then he watched her walk out of the bunkhouse and knew that his life would never be the same. He didn't know why, or how, but she'd given him something... pride? Hope? Conviction? Whatever it was, it was important. She was important. And he'd never let her down.

He wished he was there on the ranch now. He didn't like leaving her. She was older, and growing frail, but she still meant everything to him. The only reason he'd left the ranch was because she'd insisted. Otherwise, he'd be there now, overseeing her family's arrival. But he couldn't be there because he *glowered*.

Glowered indeed.

Cade snorted and began hanging up his flannel shirts in the closet, and then putting the T-shirts, jeans, socks and underwear in the dresser drawer. After putting his leather toiletry bag in the adjoining bathroom he sent Willis, the assistant ranch manager, a text. *Keep an eye on her. I'll hold you responsible if anything happens.*

Willis answered a few minutes later. *Miss Dot is in good hands.*

Cade hoped. But seeing as he wasn't at the ranch, and seeing as he was here in Marietta, he should focus on tracking down William Wyatt. But even as he turned on his iPad, he pictured blue-green eyes, a full soft mouth, and a long red ponytail gathered in a knot of red velvet, the red the same color as the paint on the exterior.

Maybe that was what had bothered him at Mrs. Bradley's house. Not all the holly jolly, but *her*.

Married or not, MerriBee Bradley was gorgeous, and married or not, he'd felt the pull of attraction, a sharp physical need that shouldn't have shocked him, but did. It had been a long time since he'd felt desire like that.

Better to hurt her feelings and leave than remain in the same house where a beautiful woman slept in a room just across from his. He was a disciplined man, but he was also a smart man. Smart men avoided unnecessary temptation.

CHAPTER TWO

MERRIBEE SURVEYED THE two dozen baskets lining the folding tables in her chilly garage. They were big baskets, and colorful, ranging from a natural wicker to baskets stained red and dark green. She collected large baskets all year long for the Christmas holiday dinners she organized and began filling them mid-November with nonperishables—cans of green beans, sweet potatoes, cranberry sauce, boxes of stuffing, jars of turkey gravy—and later she'd add a turkey or a large ham, along with fresh dinner rolls, and a just baked pie.

She usually delivered the baskets on the twenty-third, so everything would be ready in case the family wanted to celebrate their holiday meal on Christmas Eve or Christmas Day, which meant the week leading to Christmas was very hectic. She didn't mind, though, as they were her favorite days of the year. It gave her joy to see the families' joy. The recipients were grateful, and the kids were excited as the baskets didn't just include the Christmas dinner with homemade pie, they usually had holiday sweets and treats— homemade cookies, Christmas candy, and some small gifts, just little things that she wrapped but would give kids something to open Christmas morning in case Mom or Dad hadn't been able to afford something.

She'd started doing the Christmas baskets when she was in college. Initially, it was just two, after learning through her campus church that there were some families in need, and when those families still hadn't been provided for on Christmas Eve, she went to the store and filled two carts full of food and delivered them herself. She'd continued giving food baskets the next year, and the year after that. After moving to Marietta, she partnered with a local nonprofit and took on more families. She gave out of gratitude, not obligation. She'd been lucky in life, given so much, blessed with good health, a good mind, and a family that could afford to help send her to college. Education made a difference. Becoming a nurse had given her a career and a purpose. She thrived on having a purpose.

Not everyone related, though. Some people felt as if she gave too much… did too much… as if she was in competition for a volunteer of the year award. But she wanted no reward. She didn't do it for approval, or admiration. She did it because she just liked to give, and honestly, it wasn't anyone's business what she chose to do. Or not do.

CADE HAD BEEN in town two days when his hostess at the B&B mentioned the Stroll as she set a basket of warm pumpkin muffins on the big round table in the breakfast room.

"You should check it out if you can," she said. "It's an annual holiday tradition, one of the ways we kick off Christmas here. Downtown will have lots of activities. There will be carolers and hayrides, Santa, and lots of things to eat and drink."

He made a noncommittal sound because it sounded exactly like the kind of thing he avoided.

"It's going to be crowded downtown," she added, "but it's an easy walk from here. You can just walk down, look at everything, and then return home."

Two strikes against it, he thought, reaching for one of the warm muffins. "What do you do during the Stroll?" he asked. "Stroll?"

"My church has a booth. I'll be helping sell baked goods." She checked the coffee thermos on the table. "You should at least wander down, go early before it's crowded."

In the end, he did. There wasn't a lot to do in Marietta, and he was having trouble locating a William Wyatt. There was a Billy Wyatt, who'd grown up in Paradise Valley, but he'd moved away, according to the last census, and now called Utah home. There was a Wyatt ranch located in Paradise Valley but Cade wasn't sure if that was any relation to the Wyatt he was looking for. The truth was, he was struggling in his search. He didn't know how to do this—be vulnerable and put himself out there. He didn't want anyone to know his whole story. He hadn't even shared it all with Dot. He'd gotten through life by focusing on the present and working hard for the future. This dig into DNA and ancestry wasn't his thing, but at the same time, his life felt like a lie. Everything he'd been taught about himself, and his family, wasn't true. And how could he find his sister, and try to forge a relationship, if he didn't like who he was... or the family he was part of?

In his bedroom, he did another search for Wyatts of Paradise Valley, and the Marietta High School and again the name William Wyatt popped up, this time with the nickname Billy, along with a high school graduation year. William "Billy" Wyatt would be about four or five years younger than him. Cade searched again, this time using the name Billy Wyatt, and more pulled up. FFA, Marietta High School roping team, amateur cowboy champion, national amateur cowboy champion. And once the word Billy Wyatt and cowboy champion was put together, the search engine found pages and pages of mentions. The William 'Billy' Wyatt he was looking for, was a professional cowboy, and yes, he now called Utah home, but he had three brothers who lived in Montana, one still on the family ranch in Paradise Valley.

Cade closed his iPad, feeling like a dinosaur. But a somewhat satisfied dinosaur. Research wasn't his strength. He was never sure of the right words to use, never sure how to follow up on leads, but he'd made progress today. He had the address for the Wyatt ranch. He had the names of Billy's brothers. He had the ages. He even knew the name of the current owner of the ranch, Melvin Wyatt. According to the DNA results the lab had sent him, and his match on the website, William, aka Billy, had either been his uncle, his nephew, or his first cousin. Based on the year Billy graduated from high school, Cade suspected he was a cousin. But that didn't mean the rest of the family was Cade's family. It didn't mean they all shared the same DNA.

The questions were unsettling—part exciting, part nauseating. The not knowing was difficult, and he didn't want to place blame, but his mom should have been honest with him. His mom should have told him herself who his real dad was, instead of letting Cade grow up thinking Jim was his father, and then letting Jim spring the truth on him.

Jim.

James.

Jimmy O'Connell.

Hard drinker, hothead, impossible to please.

Just thinking of him made Cade's pulse quicken. His mouth tasted bitter as he walked to the bedroom window and pushed aside the navy curtain to look out his window which faced the tidy neighborhood. Mounds of snow lined the street, and trees stood like naked sentries under a steely gray sky. More snow was in the forecast, tomorrow or perhaps the day after.

Maybe he should get out, go see the town. Yesterday,

he'd driven Highway 89 south, all the way through Paradise Valley to Gardnier, the northern entrance to Yellowstone.

He stopped at a restaurant for a bison burger and coffee, and then turned around and headed back toward Marietta, taking some of the different roads in and through the mountains, wondering which of the roads led to the Wyatt ranch. Now that he had an address, he'd be able to find it easily. But what would he do when he reached the ranch? What would he say?

That was the part that held him back. He hated his ignorance. It felt like powerlessness, helplessness. He'd had enough of that as a kid.

Cade added another layer, grabbed his coat and hat, and walked the four blocks to Main Street, which had already been blocked up with barricades on all side streets, turning Main Street into a pedestrian-only zone. At one end he could see the big red brick courthouse with its snow-dusted dome. Behind the dome rose Copper Mountain, low clouds obscuring the peak. In the other direction it was just shops, and white canvas booths, with folks decorating plain folding tables, turning them into festive displays.

He stopped in at Java Café for a coffee to go, and as he exited the café, he spotted a woman with a long red ponytail, the tip of the ponytail reaching almost to her butt.

His gut tightened as he recognized the petite frame, the delicate profile, and the glowing hair. She was carrying huge plastic tubs, two of them, stacked on top of each other. She couldn't see where she was going and had to stop more than once to peek around the tubs.

Cade quickened his stride, reaching her as she started walking again.

"Put those down," he said.

Her head snapped back and she looked up at him, bewildered, and then seeing it was him, her brows pulled into a frown. "Is that how you speak to everyone, Mr. Hunt? I have to say, it's not very charming."

Of course she'd be difficult. "*Please* put those down. I'll take the tubs, if you take my coffee."

"I'm fine."

"You have a man offering help, please accept his help."

She was craning her neck in order to look him in the eye. "Yes, but I don't need a man's help, and I didn't ask for your help, so you're not doing me a favor. You're just getting in my way."

He wasn't in the mood to argue. He wasn't in a good mood in the first place. He set his coffee on the curb and just took the tubs from her. She resisted and for a second they were both tugging in opposite directions before he won, because of course he'd win, he was physically stronger.

"That wasn't fair," she said, using a crimson mitten to push a fiery-red tendril from her forehead. "It's not chivalrous to outmuscle a woman."

Her cheeks were a dark pink, and her full lips drew his attention, and the fierceness in her eyes intrigued him more than it should. She was irritated with him, but it didn't bother him. He'd rather her be mad than carry heavy bins. And while the big plastic tubs weren't a strain for him, they were large and awkward to carry. "Lead the way."

"Did you hear anything I said?" she demanded.

"I did."

Her eyebrows arched. "And?"

"I don't know where to take these."

There were more flinty lights in her eyes, deepening the color. She had beautiful eyes, blues and greens with a fleck of violet in one.

She made a low rough sound of disgust in her throat and grabbed his coffee off the curb and set off, marching briskly down the street to a pair of folding tables with more bins pushed beneath them. "Here," she said, sweeping an arm at her area. "You may place them here."

He set them on the table and took his coffee back. "Do you have more?"

"No, those were the last." Her chin lifted, her lips compressed. "Mr. Hunt, I hope you know those tubs are filled with holiday cheer."

He wanted to smile, amused. She reminded him of his favorite hot sauce—spicy and sweet, a hint of vinegar, a dash of cayenne pepper. The corner of his mouth tugged. "As long as the cheer is safely entombed, Mrs. Bradley, we're okay."

She gave him a long, assessing glance before removing the lid of one tub, revealing strings of white lights. "I will be freeing the cheer very quickly. I have a lot to do and am running short on time, so you'd better run before all my festivity drags you under."

"Why are you running behind?"

"I couldn't find my hand trolley, and I had to park farther away than I expected. It was a lot of trips back and forth."

"There's no one to help you?"

"No."

"What about Mr. Bradley?"

She hesitated for just a fraction of a second, as if uncertain how to answer. "He's gone."

"As in out of town?"

"As in gone-gone. John died five years ago."

Cade stiffened, wincing inwardly at his inept handling of her, and this conversation. "I'm sorry."

"Thank you. He was a lovely man."

Cade shouldn't have come down here. Shouldn't be on Main Street with its candy cane lights and festive decorations. Or standing near this slip of a woman with hair so glossy he wanted to touch it and see what it felt like. "I feel terrible," he said, because he did. He felt rude, and hostile.

"It's a simple mistake," she answered, giving him a smile that was almost kind, a first from her today. "It happens all the time."

He couldn't continue this conversation and he didn't know how to extract himself. "How will you be hanging the lights?"

She looked up and then down the street at other tables. "Last year we had poles. I just wrapped the lights on that." Her frown deepened as she saw other tables had poles. "Some people have them." Then she looked at the ground, and crouched down to check under the tables. "I don't even have an electrical outlet. It was supposed to be included in my setup."

"Let me go check out what others have," he said.

"No one will be able to see my things without lights."

"I'll make sure you have light."

"How?" she asked, a thread of panic making her voice rise.

"I keep a portable generator in my truck. It will easily power your lights for the evening." He saw her expression start to clear. "It's going to be okay, I promise."

"You don't happen to have poles to hang my lights on, do you?" she said, with a rueful smile.

Her mouth was made for kissing. Her face lit up when she laughed. He couldn't remember the last time he'd felt this attracted to anyone. "I can put something together. Leave it to me."

"I thought you hated decorations."

"Yes, but I can be flexible when necessary."

"It *is* a good cause," she assured him.

"Then I'll make some magic happen."

She studied him for a long moment, clearly hopeful but

also wary. "You're serious about helping me?"

He shrugged. "I have nothing else to do."

"You flatterer, you," she teased.

Cade choked on a muffled laugh, the heaviness within him easing. He had something to do, and someone in need of help, and he knew how to help. All in all, he felt better than he had in days. Probably since leaving the ranch.

A HALF HOUR later, MerriBee surveyed her booth. She had a tall wooden frame wrapped in hundreds of white lights, with more fairy lights strung across the front of the tables. Her sign, *John's Heart*, hung squarely in the middle of the upper railing. Her tables were draped with a rich purple-blue velvet and her knitted items were arranged on the tables, with additional stock below in the tubs.

"It's never looked this good," she said to Cade, who still had a power tool in his hand. He'd brought his whole toolbox from his truck and even made a trip to the lumber-yard. "Thank you," she said, smiling at him. "I think this is going to be my best year yet."

"I see a lot of knitted things."

She nodded. "Scarves, caps, some blankets, small ones for kids, and large ones for adults." She ran a light hand over one of the soft fuzzy blankets wrapped with a ribbon. "I like the small ones as they make the perfect size lap blanket when I'm watching TV."

"Who made these?"

"I make most of them, although I do get some made for me to sell."

"Is that what you do, knit and run the B&B?"

She looked at him, baffled. "No, I'm a nurse. I knit when my patients sleep, gives me something to do when they're resting but they still want me close."

He now looked confused. "You're a nurse?"

"A hospice nurse," she said.

"I had no idea."

"I don't think we ever had a chance to talk before." She smiled at him. "My house terrified you."

"Your house is fine. I'm just… me."

Her smile stretched. "You're fine, too. I think we're all fine now."

His laugh was a low rumble, and it struck her that he probably didn't laugh very often. "So, what do you do with the money you raise?"

"I make Christmas baskets for families in the community. Our local yarn store donates the yarn, I turn the yarn into blankets and scarves, and when I sell everything tonight, I'll use the cash to buy whatever I don't yet have for the baskets. Some years it's for extra turkeys and ham. Other years it's presents for kids. Just depends."

A gust of wind caught at the frame, making it sway a little. Cade went behind the tables to check the sturdiness, giving the wood a shake. He'd taken his coat off to work, and was wearing a navy plaid wool shirt, the navy relieved by thin butter-yellow lines. It was an older shirt, worn, but it looked comfortable, the sturdy fabric outlined the width of his back, and hugged his biceps and triceps. "It could use some weights to anchor it better."

"I don't suppose you have any sandbags in your truck?"

He flashed her a faint smile over his shoulder. "I don't, but I can put my toolbox on one side and figure something out for the other side." He looked around them, his gaze lingering on the bookstore on the opposite corner. "Books might work."

"Let's not do that. I say we just go for it. I think we're going to be alright. It shouldn't get much windier than it is now."

He pulled out his phone. "I'm going to text you my number. Call me during the Stroll if you need anything. I can always come back and just sit on the thing to weigh it down."

"Okay, but I think I'll be fine."

"What's your number?" he asked.

She rattled off her number, which he input into his contacts, before calling her once. He glanced up at her. "What time should I be back to help you break down?"

She opened her mouth to protest, and then realized she wanted his help. "Ten," she said. "At least that's the official end time. I suppose if I sell out earlier, I could pack up."

"I'll be back at nine thirty, but if you need me earlier,

just call."

She nodded, cheeks growing warm, because he wasn't John, and yet she felt that intense awareness again, as if they'd met before, as if he was familiar. But obviously they hadn't met, and obviously he wasn't familiar.

She studied his face, her eyes searching his, then sweeping over his strong, masculine features. She wanted to understand, wanted to identify whatever this was she was feeling so she could contain the emotions, minimize the threat. "I keep thinking I've met you. But we haven't, have we?"

"No," he said, and then grabbing his coat and hat from the folding chair, he walked away.

A frisson of pleasure coursed down her spine. Cade Hunt was very much a man, a fit, virile man, and watching him walk away before her insides did a somersault, and her pulse raced. She had the strangest feeling he was going to change things, but how, she didn't yet know.

IT WAS NEARLY dark when Cade left MerriBee to work her table, and people had begun to fill Main Street. In the distance, he heard singing, and a big horse pulling a trailer filled with hay bales clip clopped down toward the courthouse. The Marietta Stroll was coming to life before his eyes. He hadn't wanted to participate, but here he was, on his own, and hungry, too.

He hesitated bothering MerriBee but he wondered if she'd be able to recommend a good place for dinner, so he texted her the question, aware that she might not even see the text.

She did, though, and answered right away. *The diner is great for everything. There's a Mexican restaurant before the diner on the right side. You can get Italian on Church, Chinese on Front Street, and the old Bank of Marietta is now a fancy steak house. Haven't been there yet but heard it was good, if you want a good steak.*

Thanks, he texted back. *I'll try the steak house.*

Cade ate dinner sitting at the counter in the bar of the steak house in the turn-of-the-century bank. This steak house was fancy, with more marble and rich polished wood than he was comfortable with, but the steak was excellent, and the beer was cold.

As he ate, Cade thought about this Billy Wyatt who was supposed to be his cousin. Cade had never had a cousin before, and he'd never known anyone on his real father's side before. He was eager to meet Billy, eager to know more, but also aware that Billy might not reciprocate the feelings. The Wyatts might not want or need an outsider pushing his way in.

The bartender, a young man, with dark, nearly black hair, and a strong, clean-shaven jaw checked in on Cade where he sat at the counter. "Anything else I can get you?" he asked. "Another beer?"

Cade shook his head. "I'm good, thanks."

The young man eyed him with interest. "Are you new here? Or just traveling through?"

"A little of both," Cade answered. "Here for a few weeks, and then back home to Wyoming."

"Nice. Most tourists come in summertime, so this time of year it's mainly locals, but Marietta is festive. We have a lot of Christmas spirit here."

"I've noticed." Cade glanced at his phone. No text or call yet from MerriBee. "What about you?" he asked the bartender. "Are you a local?"

"Grew up in Paradise Valley. I'm attending college in Bozeman now. I'm in my last year there. Need to save up money, hoping to go to law school."

"Good for you."

The bartender shrugged. "I like law. I didn't want to be a sheriff or a policeman. I figured with a degree in criminal science, and then a law degree, I'd have a lot of options, but I'm getting tired of school."

"I had a hard time in school. You're smart to stick with it."

"My mom believed education is the way you get ahead. Hope she's right," the bartender said, placing the bill on the counter in front of Cade.

"Your mom sounds like a wise woman."

"I think she was. I never really knew her. She died when I was a baby."

"I'm sorry."

"It was twenty-one years ago. I don't even know why I mentioned it."

Cade was intrigued though. "You grew up in Paradise Valley?"

The young man nodded. "My dad has a cattle ranch."

"You didn't want to be a rancher?"

"No, and I don't think he wants me to follow in his footsteps. Now my sister, she might. She's a cowgirl to the core."

Cade picked up the bill, glanced at the number at the bottom. A thought struck him. He looked up at the bartender still standing there. "Have you ever heard of a family by the name of Wyatt? They have some property in Paradise Valley, too."

"Of course I do. They're famous around here."

"Are they? Why?"

"The Wyatt brothers are world-class cowboys. They're professional rodeo cowboys. Sam didn't make nationals this year, but Billy and Tommy are in Vegas now."

"So Billy's not going to be around here now."

"No, sir. But he'll be back after the NFRs. The family always comes together for Christmas."

"Sounds like you know them pretty well."

"Their ranch is about fifteen minutes from my granddad's place." He reached for a cocktail napkin, scribbled down a number. "If you need anything, or want an introduction, my dad would be happy to help you. My dad's Brock Sheenan, and I'm Mack." Mack handed over the cocktail napkin. "I've got finals coming up so I'm going to be in Bozeman next week studying, but then I'll be back. In the meantime, my dad knows everyone, and so does Harley."

"Harley?" Cade repeated, pocketing the cocktail napkin.

"My stepmom, but she's like my mom. She's awesome."

Mack Sheenan moved down the counter to fill a new drink order. Cade slipped some bills out of his wallet, and tucked them under his empty glass. He then thought about it, and added an extra twenty for the bartender, respecting his work ethic. "Have a good night," Cade said, standing.

Mack tipped his head. "You, too."

It was cold outside, the strong, biting wind stinging Cade's neck. He pulled up the collar of his jacket to protect his nape. He was glad for his hat, and dragged it down on his head to keep it from blowing off.

Main Street was still crowded. The booths lining both sides of the street were still busy. He walked down the middle of the street, hands in his pockets, watching people, listening to laughter and conversation. Somewhere he could hear carolers sing.

It really was too bad that holidays made him uneasy, because there was a certain charm to this small Montana town, where everyone smiled and nodded as you walked by.

He returned to his starting point, outside the bank turned steak house, and watched MerriBee talk to some customers. Her cheeks were pink, her eyes bright. The tip of her nose glowed red. She looked happy, and her two tables were nearly bare, surprisingly depleted. She said she hoped to sell everything, and it looked like she was pretty close to doing that. Good for her.

MerriBee spotted him and waved him over. He gave his head a slight shake, seeing that she was still speaking with a couple. She nodded at him, and waved again, insistent. Again, he shook his head and her smile faded a little but she accepted his refusal.

Cade wasn't sure how much longer she'd be, so he crossed the street, entered the bookstore on the corner. He wasn't big on books, but Dot loved to read. Maybe he could find something for her, for Christmas. He wandered around the store, feeling out of place. He'd never enjoyed reading. Stories weren't an escape for him. Even as a boy, he hadn't liked fairy tales, or made-up stories. He didn't see any point in imagining anything. Why pretend? It did nothing. Life was hard. Pretending didn't make it any easier.

Cade left the bookstore, restless.

He glanced at MerriBee's booth and saw she was beginning to pack up. Of course she was. It'd kill her to ask him for help. Stubborn woman.

He suppressed a sigh and headed over. "You were supposed to call," he said, reaching her side.

"You wouldn't come over," she said. "I wanted you to meet my friends, Sophie and Joe Wyatt."

"Wyatt?" he repeated numbly.

She nodded. "They have a ranch in Paradise Valley. Sophie's become a good friend of mine. This year she knitted a dozen scarves for me to sell, and we sold out of everything."

"That's wonderful," he said, trying to remember what the couple looked like, and coming up blank. He should have walked over. He wished he'd met Joe Wyatt. He could at least have found out if he was Billy Wyatt's brother. Hopefully, there would be another opportunity, and soon.

Chapter Three

A FTER LOADING UP her car, Cade had offered to meet her at her house and carry everything in, but MerriBee had refused. He had done more than his share tonight, and she could easily take the empty tubs into the garage tomorrow.

It had been a successful night, and she was pleased by the amount of money she'd earned. Joe Wyatt had given her two one-hundred-dollar bills as a donation for her baskets. She'd been touched, and she was still delighted, but also cold, and ready for a warm bath and bed.

Teeth chattering, she jumped out of her car, grabbed her purse and slammed the car door closed. She dashed up the sidewalk, noting that some of the bulbs around the windows had burned out. She needed to get those changed. She was just about to step up, when her foot landed on ice. The patch was wide and slick and she had too much momentum. MerriBee went sailing forward, hands flying out as if she could break the fall. She couldn't, and she slammed into the steps, her head knocking against the bricks as she went down.

For a moment she was too dazed to think. For a moment she couldn't even move. It hurt to breathe and pain washed through her, the pain everywhere... in her head, the wrist she'd landed on, the leg twisted beneath her.

She reached out to touch the side of her head, just off her temple. Her fingers came away wet. She looked at them and they were covered in blood. As a nurse, she knew head wounds bled a lot, so the cut might not be very deep, but it also might mean stitches. She struggled to sit up and went woozy with pain. Her wrist was bad. She gingerly explored her left wrist. Something was out of place, probably broken. She tried to stand, but the pain shooting through her ankle was unbearable, and she crumpled back down, falling onto her backside. Goodness, how much damage had she done?

Tears stung her eyes. She could feel the dampness on her head, feel the cold air blow against her scalp. She touched the cut again, and this time she could feel skin—no longer attached. Oh, dumb, dumb, dumb. She should have salted her sidewalk before heading out. She shouldn't have been rushing. There was no reason for it. She'd lived in Marietta for years now, and she'd grown up in Spokane. She knew all about ice—black ice, shiny white ice, snow-covered ice.

Thankfully MerriBee was practical and not prone to dramatics. So, after a moment of silently beating herself up, she wiped her hand on her jeans then reached into her coat pocket for her phone. Who should she call? She tried to think of a neighbor she could bother, but it didn't seem right. She was friendly with all, but not close to anyone, and Sophie, who was a friend, lived almost thirty minutes away in the mountains.

She could call an ambulance but the last thing she wanted to do was show up at her hospital in an ambulance with a twisted ankle. That would be beyond humiliating. She was supposed to be one of their ace nurses. She didn't need an ambulance; she just needed a ride to the ER.

She needed someone who wouldn't make a big fuss to take her there. Someone who'd just get the job done.

Cade Hunt.

He'd do it.

She told Siri to call Cade Hunt on speaker, and her phone did. She hoped Cade would be available, she hoped he'd answer, but she wasn't sure. However, he did take the call, and very calmly she explained that she'd taken a fall, and was on her front steps bleeding, and if he wouldn't mind, she'd appreciate a ride to the hospital. She stopped talking and took a breath. "If it's not too inconvenient," she added in a small voice.

"On my way," he answered, before hanging up.

And he was. Cade arrived in his 1972 Chevy in less than a minute, sheepskin coat open, hat on his head. He parked behind her car in the driveway, left the engine running, and scooped her up in his arms as if she weighed nothing.

"What hurts?" he asked, carrying her to the passenger side, where he managed to open the door without jiggling her too much.

He'd felt strong and warm, and she immediately missed his warmth as he deposited her carefully on the seat. "A little bit of everything," she said, wincing as she tried to adjust her foot. "My left side took the brunt of the fall, and I hit my head hard on the step. It's bleeding, might need stitches. My wrist feels funny, could be broken. I tried to stand, but didn't push it."

He tugged on the seat belt, extending it, before securing her. "How did you fall?"

"Rushed up the sidewalk, slipped on ice."

"That's an amateur move, Bradley," he said, shutting her door and coming around to the driver's side.

She huffed a soft laugh. "Tell me about it. That's why I didn't want to call an ambulance. Can you imagine me showing up, to my own medical facility, in an ambulance for a sprained ankle?"

"I'm glad you called me then."

She was, too, especially when they reached the hospital and rather than wait for assistance, Cade again lifted her into his arms, carried her into the ER, and said she needed help.

MerriBee didn't think she looked bad, but when the nurse at the desk saw her, she immediately gestured for Cade to take MerriBee into a room. "We'll get you looked at right away," she said.

A nurse came in to MerriBee's room, took vitals, briefly looked at the wound, made notes in the chart, and said that someone would be with her soon before disappearing with a swish through the fabric curtain.

MerriBee was still in her coat, on the bed, and she reached into her pocket for her phone, and turned the camera on, pivoting it into selfie mode. Using the camera as a mirror, she took a good look at herself. Blood matted her head. Her scalp was hanging off at a weird angle, more blood streaked down the side of her face, her neck, disappearing into the collar of her sweater. "I look a little bit like Carrie from the prom scene."

"When she gets drenched in pig's blood?"

"The very one." MerriBee turned off her phone and looked at Cade who was standing to the side of her bed. "There's more skin hanging off than I thought."

"You sliced it open pretty good," he said.

"I will need stitches."

"Does that scare you?"

"They'll numb me up and then it should be okay." She tried to sound casual and brave, but the truth was, she didn't much like getting shots, and she'd never had stitches before. She couldn't imagine having her scalp sewn closed. Which made her remember her nursing training. Rinse wound, if on scalp, shave where necessary, clean wound again. Suture. "How many stitches do you think?"

He leaned over her, gently lifted some of the hair from her head, inspecting the wound. "The gash is at least two to three inches long. I imagine they'll want some staples in there, along with the stitches."

"How do you know this stuff?"

"My ranch hands get hurt regularly. We don't even bother with the ER most of the time. We just fix them up in the office."

"Who is we?" she asked.

"Willis—the assistant ranch manager, his wife Em, and me." He gently settled her hair back and went to wash his hands in the sink, but not before she saw the blood on them. "Personally, I'm a fan of superglue. Mends most things."

"Like what?" she asked, watching him soap his hands and then dry them on a paper towel.

"Fingers, elbows, cheekbones, jaws, chins." He tossed the paper towel away, gave her a concerned look. "How's the pain right now?"

"Eh, okay." She glanced at the curtain. The shock was beginning to wear off and fear was setting in. "Do you think they'll shave my head? For the stitches?"

A doctor entered the room, and he immediately recognized MerriBee. "What are you doing here, MerriBee? I thought this was the month you took some time off. Missed us already?"

"Oh, you know me, Dr. McCarthy, I can't seem to get enough of Marietta Medical."

"Weren't you at the Stroll tonight? You usually have a booth there."

"I did," she answered. "This happened when I got

home."

"What did happen?"

"Ran up a sidewalk covered in ice."

"That will do it every time." Dr. McCarthy glanced at her chart again then checked her head wound, and examined her arms, legs, and then titled her head back to look at her eyes. "Did you lose consciousness?"

"No."

"Are you dizzy? How's your vision?"

"There is only one of you."

He smiled. "That's good. But you could have a concussion so we're going to want to keep an eye on that. In the meantime, we'll take some X-rays, see what we're dealing with, and then I'll have the nurse come back, clean you up, and then I'll close your head up."

She forced a smile. "I'll be here."

Dr. McCarthy stepped out, and a young man came in to wheel her down to imaging. She looked at Cade, who'd been silent ever since the doctor arrived. "Are you okay?" she asked him.

"I'm fine."

"If you're bored—"

"I'll be here when you get back."

She closed her eyes as the orderly pushed her bed down the softly lit hall, and it was a surprisingly long trip, where they went right and then left, and up in the elevator several floors. She was feeling sleepy and left her eyes closed as they took the pictures they wanted. She didn't even realize she'd fallen asleep until she was back in her cubicle in the ER and another nurse had come in to "clean her up," which meant pouring a pitcher of water over her scalp to wash out the dried blood. The water wasn't very warm and there was a lot of water coming down, an entire pitcher full, soaking her shoulders, and the back of her sweater.

MerriBee's teeth began chattering. She was drenched all the way through, and she suddenly just wanted to be home, and warm, and dry. Instead, she was under glaringly bright lights, cold, wet, and miserable.

"She could use a towel," Cade said, his voice breaking the silence.

"What's that?" the nurse said.

"She's soaking wet. Can you get her a towel?"

"Oh, sure." The young nurse disappeared and returned a minute later with some towels. "Sorry about all that water," she said, sliding one beneath MerriBee's shoulders, and covering her chest with the other. "I've never had to do this before. The doctor said get it really clean, but there was so much blood."

As miserable as she was, MerriBee understood. "You're doing great," MerriBee reassured the girl. "I bet you've got most of the blood out now."

"I think so." The nurse smiled shyly. "I heard you were Mrs. B, or MerriBee, from the palliative ward. Dr. McCarthy said you're the best nurse on that ward."

"He's being kind," MerriBee answered.

"No, he said you took care of his mom as she was dying. He said you were like an angel."

MerriBee's eyes burned. That had been years ago, in her first year caring for those in hospice. She hadn't thought Dr. McCarthy would remember.

"She was a lovely lady," MerriBee said, keeping the corners of her lips up so she couldn't cry. She suddenly felt too much, simply everything, and after a long year, followed by the stress of the Stroll, her emotions felt overwhelming.

"Did you start out in hospice?" the young nurse asked.

"No," MerriBee answered hoarsely. "After my husband died, I realized that it was something I could do that others didn't want to do, and I've been in palliative care ever since."

The nurse patted MerriBee's damp shoulder. "I think you're brave."

MerriBee blinked, and a small tear fell. "Not brave. It's just what I'm called to do."

The nurse stepped out of the room, and the curtain swished, and then all was silent for a minute.

Cade's deep voice broke the silence. "Sounds like you're a hero around here."

She'd forgotten he was there. He'd been so quiet all this time. She reached up and wiped away the tear then turned her head to better see him. "What time is it?"

"Eleven forty-five."

"And they haven't even started sewing yet."

"It's going to be another couple hours before you're out of here, especially if they need to set anything."

She looked down at her left wrist. It was swollen and discolored. "Like this thing?"

"I could set it for you, but since we're here, why not let the professionals do the job?"

Despite the pain, and the fatigue, she smiled. "You're funny."

"Not really."

"No, you are. You just have a very dry sense of humor."

"So dry some people don't think I have any."

She lay back against the pillow, everything still wet from her bath. "I appreciate a nice dry sense of humor, especially as I'm still soaked."

He grabbed the chair from the corner and placed it next to the bed. "I thought she was trying to drown you."

MerriBee laughed softly. "Someone should probably work with her on technique."

"You should have her come work with you. I have a feeling you could teach her a lot."

"Palliative care isn't for everyone. We have a lot of staff that rotates out, unable to handle it long term. Let's face it, death isn't something our society prepares us for. Most of us spend our life avoiding it, fighting to stay young, fighting to feel useful, powerful. Death is just the opposite."

"How have you handled it?"

She pictured John, and her chest ached. She'd been there

for him out of love. And she'd cared for the others out of love, too. She didn't know how to talk about it. She didn't want to try to explain it. It was just her work, and she could do it, provided she took off three or four weeks every year to unplug, recharge, reset. As she was doing now. "I just find a balance," she said at length. "I take December off every year. It's the month where I don't work. I take all my vacation and personal time and do different things, and then come January, I'm ready to get back to work."

"Most nurses are trained to save people."

"I started as a nurse in the neonatal unit, caring for the preemies, babies fighting for their lives, but after meeting John, I realized that there needed to be people who were fighting at the end of life, for one's quality of life. We should have wonderful people welcoming us into the world, and equally wonderful people helping us leave."

HER WORDS WERE warm, but they left him cold, and Cade shifted in his chair, uncomfortable. His mom hadn't left the world the way MerriBee described. His mom's death hadn't been filled with warmth, or tenderness. She hadn't had loving people, much less loving family, around her. Cade certainly hadn't been there for her as he should have, too immature and selfish to understand that fighting with Jimmy wouldn't bring her any comfort. Jimmy hadn't cared for her, either, spending no time with her while she died, his affection absent for years. Her medical care had been equally apathetic, making her final days filled with needless pain and suffering.

At eighteen, he hadn't known what to do, or how to fix the situation. He hadn't realized there were other options, better options, than simply suffering, as she had, begging for someone to put her out of her misery and just let her die.

But no one had. And Cade hated remembering.

He lurched to his feet, livid with himself all over again. His memories were never good ones. There was so little love and laughter to remember, so little love for any of them. "I left my phone in the truck," he said curtly. "I'm going to go get it. Do you want anything?"

She shook her head but he didn't do more than glance her way before exiting her cubicle and then through the ER doors to the waiting room. He nodded at the nurse at the desk and headed outside.

The night was frigid and he shivered at a gust of icy wind, the wind rifling through his hair, making his eyes sting and water. He'd left his coat in MerriBee's cubicle but he didn't mind the cold. The cold would soon clear his head, settle his thoughts.

He wished he could think of his mom without getting upset, but pain and anger were so tightly woven that he felt both every time he thought of her, whether living or dead. His mom hadn't been a bad person but she'd had problems, and she'd chosen the wrong partner. Jim drank, she took pills and did whatever else she could do to numb herself, and together they were as dysfunctional as they came. They split up, got back together, split up, got back together, and every time they split up, Cade prayed and prayed his mom wouldn't take Jim back. Cade didn't care if Jim was his father. Jim was rotten to the core and even as a boy, Cade knew he and his mom were better off without him.

But his mom was as addicted to Jim as she was her pills, and apparently life with an abusive husband was better than life without him. Cade didn't get it, and her weakness made him despise her. And then she got sick and she never got better.

She died the way she lived—broken.

Jim had been too drunk the day of her funeral to do anything but embarrass himself, talking over the priest, insulting guests who'd come, laughing at Cade, telling him his mom was a whore. The only thing that got Cade through the graveside service was knowing he was finally free to leave home permanently. He could return to Sundowner Ranch, or join the army, or do both, because now with Mom gone, he had no problem walking away from his dad forever.

Cade didn't think he'd been outside all that long, but when he returned to MerriBee's room, her eyes were watery. "What's wrong?" he asked.

"Dr. McCarthy has gone to get the clippers to shave my head—"

"He doesn't have to shave your head."

"He said it's the best way to close it properly without infection."

Cade didn't agree. He'd taken a young guest and her grandmother to the hospital before, after the girl got kicked by a horse and needed stitches. The girl had long blonde hair and the doctor hadn't shaved her head. He'd cleaned it well, and then closed the wound with staples. Cade didn't know why Dr. McCarthy couldn't do the same. "I'll speak to him."

"He'll say it's hospital protocol."

"Yes, but there must be some leeway for patients' wishes." He reached down and touched her shoulder, his fingertips brushing her wet hair that was starting to dry, turning into long ringlets. "Let me see what I can do."

"Dr. McCarthy will say it's his ER."

Cade smiled at her. "And I'll remind him it's your Marietta Medical."

MERRIBEE WATCHED CADE step past the curtain again, and she felt a whoosh of emotion—loss, regret, confusion. She wasn't exactly sure what she felt, only she hadn't wanted him to leave her, not again. She felt safe with him there. Protected. She couldn't remember the last time she'd had anyone taking care of her… not that she needed care, not normally. But in this instance, it felt good. Cade was tough and had a hard side, but he was also skilled at managing problems, as well as handling people.

She liked his confidence, and respected his ability to take charge. His authority had irritated her in her own home, but it was welcome here.

He returned five minutes later, pulled the chair close and sat town. "He's not going to shave your head. He's putting the clippers away."

Without thinking, she reached for his hand, gave it a quick grateful squeeze. "That's wonderful."

"But he's also not going to do the work, either," Cade added. "He disagrees with the decision but has spoken with Dr. Gallagher, and Dr. Gallagher agrees that it's not necessary, so he'll close the wound with a combination of staples and stitches. The stitches will dissolve, but you'll need to see your doctor in seven to ten days to have the staples removed."

"That really is great news."

"Not so great news? Your wrist is broken so you'll need a cast and then your ankle wrapped. That's not broken. You just have a bad sprain, but it will mean crutches for you, which won't be easy with a cast on your wrist."

She'd watched his face the entire time he talked, her eyes searching his, trying to see past the pale blue of his irises, wanting to see more of who he was, and what he thought, and believed. He didn't open up much, and even after a night in his company she knew virtually nothing about him.

"That does sound tricky," she said, aware of the late hour and the treatments ahead of her. Of them. Because he was here, too, spending his night in the hospital with her. "I'm sorry to have dragged you into this."

"I'm not," he said bluntly. "I'm glad I was available. I've been trying to figure out who would have helped you if I hadn't."

She didn't immediately answer, because there wasn't really anyone she knew who would have dropped everything and come to her assistance. Well, that wasn't true. Sophie would come, but Sophie lived outside town and had two very young children. MerriBee had gotten to know Taylor Sheenan, Marietta's head librarian, but Taylor also had a family, and MerriBee didn't want to ask moms and wives to drop everything. It made her uncomfortable asking for help when they already had so much on their plate. "I'm not sure," she said at last.

"So, who helps you when you need help?" he persisted.

MerriBee was tired and she hurt and they still hadn't given her anything for the pain. She didn't feel like playing word games with Cade, or for that matter, any kind of game. "I'm usually pretty self-sufficient," she said, even as the curtain swished open to admit a doctor and a nurse. "I've never been hurt before."

"But when your car breaks down, or you need a hand, don't you have girlfriends you can call?"

"I try not to need things," she said simply. "It's easier that way."

CHAPTER FOUR

I T WAS ALMOST three in the morning when MerriBee was finally discharged and Cade drove her home. He carried her into the house, and when he started for the stairs, she pointed down the hall, to the bedroom she sometimes used as her craft room. "I think I'd better stay downstairs. It will be easier for me to be independent down here."

He changed direction, carrying her into the bedroom, pausing to allow MerriBee to turn on the lights. A large folding table took up a big portion of the room, the table covered in wrapping paper and ribbons and bows. She heard him sigh at the sight, and she sighed in return. "It's just wrapping paper," she said.

He carefully set her on the edge of the bed. "Can I move any of it for you?"

"It's not in my way."

He nodded once, walked out, returning a few minutes later with her crutches and prescriptions, setting the paper bag on the nightstand, and leaning the crutches against the side of the bed.

"Anything else? Pajamas, toothbrush, phone charger?" he

asked.

"I have a charger in here. But I'd love something clean to sleep in, and yes, to my toothbrush as well." She told him how to find both, and she listened as he climbed the back stairs to reach her room.

He wasn't gone very long, appearing relatively quickly with a matched pajama set, her electric toothbrush and toothpaste, along with a bottle of facial cleanser. MerriBee was impressed, and surprised. "You did well," she said.

He gave her an indecipherable look. "I've had girlfriends, Mrs. Bradley."

Something in his dry tone and something in that long, penetrating look, made her flush, and squirm a bit. It was as if he was saying he was just as experienced as her, except, she wasn't experienced. She wasn't good at relationships at all.

"Do you need help changing?" he asked.

"I'm good. I can manage the rest. Go home and get sleep. I'll be fine now."

"I don't think you should be left alone, not after everything you've been through."

"I promise I'll be okay. I just want to go to bed and I'm sure you're desperate for sleep as well." She glanced at her wristwatch. "It's nearly three thirty. Tomorrow will be here before we know it."

"I'm going to stick around. You have a concussion."

"I'm fine. If I'd had an adverse reaction I think we'd know by now."

"I'm not leaving."

"I'll call you when I wake up."

He shrugged, as if to say he was done arguing. "Sure."

❦

SHE HOPPED INTO the bathroom next to the downstairs bedroom, not bothering with the crutches, and then when finished, hopped and hobbled back to the bedroom, closed the door, and after a moment's hesitation, locked the door. She felt a little vulnerable tonight. She didn't like being hurt. With just one good arm and one good leg, she wouldn't be very good in a fight to the finish. Hopefully tonight there would be nothing dangerous she had to fight.

MerriBee made a face and carefully climbed in the bed where a small table lamp burned, the cranberry glass glowing pink. This room had some of her favorite antiques, the tall carved walnut headboard for the queen-size bed, and a tall matching dresser against the wall. Everything in this room was pretty, furnished from either an antique store or bought at an estate sale. She called it the rose room, because of the pink glass on the antique lamp, the soft dark pink throw on the foot of the bed, and a small watercolor of violets and pink roses she'd framed and hung on the wall. She'd found the watercolor—no bigger than the lid of a children's shoebox—at an antique store and had fallen in love with it immediately. Someone had labored over it years ago. Had it been a gift for someone? Had it been painted to remember the flowers, perhaps a gift from a beloved?

MerriBee turned off the light and settled back, scooting into the soft pillows. She loved her old house, and loved her life. She knew she was a bit out of step with other women her age, women who were marrying and having children. But she had her own mission, and she was happy with her choices... mostly. She'd always assumed she'd have a family, but it hadn't happened, and it was hard to picture herself falling in love again. Loving had proven painful. But it was at night, when she wondered what life would have been like if John had been healthy, and they'd had a baby. Would she be working so hard at the hospital? Would she and John be in Marietta today? Or would they be somewhere else, perhaps living in a resort town in Big Sky or the Grand Tetons, and he'd be a ski instructor, and in his free time he'd teach their babies how to fly down the slopes, too? At night they'd talk with the lights out, and he'd hold her hand over the covers, and she'd tell him about her day, both good and bad, and he'd listen, because he was good at that. She wondered what it would feel like to have a partner in crime, someone who got her, someone who cared, not just with hello and good-bye, but with the real stuff, the big, heavy stuff.

She'd never shared any of the big, heavy stuff with John. Because as much as she had loved him—and oh, she'd loved him—she'd always tried to protect him, to shield him from her insecurities, and her fear. She didn't want him to ever worry about her or feel guilty that he couldn't do more with her, or for her.

MerriBee turned once at night, forgetting her ankle, and the pain shocked her into wakefulness. She hurt all over, but her ankle throbbed. Her wrist ached. She reached over to the nightstand and struggled to open the pill bottle one-handed, only to realize she had no water in the room. She should have brought a glass in with her last night. Her eyes burned with frustration. If she didn't hurt so much, she wouldn't bother, but she did hurt. Blinking back tears of frustration, she limped out of her room, into the bathroom across the hall, and stuck her head under the faucet to drink, swallowing the pill. She banged her wrist as she climbed back into bed, and her eyes stung with fresh tears. This was so stupid. She didn't like being hurt. She didn't want to be the patient, and not at the start of her vacation.

It took at least twenty minutes for the pill to provide any relief, but eventually the throbbing eased and MerriBee fell back asleep.

Opening her door three hours later, sun streamed through a window in the hall. The house was warm and she could smell coffee brewing. Or brewed.

She used the rest room and then hobbled and hopped down the hallway toward the kitchen. But as she passed the living room she saw a fire crackling brightly in the big fireplace. She never built a fire, not for herself, but it burned cheerfully now, and the lights on the Christmas tree were on, too. Baffled, she gave her head a slight shake.

"Morning," a deep masculine voice spoke.

She leaned more heavily on the crutch and turned to look at Cade. "How did you get in?"

"I took the silver train key ring with me last night so that I could move myself back in."

There were so many pieces to process she didn't even know where to start.

He seemed to understand as he helpfully suggested she find a comfortable chair in the living room and said he'd bring her coffee. "How do you like it?" he asked.

"A splash oh half-and-half, and two of those artificial sweeteners in the tea cupboard," she said, unable to move. "But I can make it—"

"You could, but you can't carry it, so go sit, and I'll fix you a cup and bring it to you. We have lots to cover."

She didn't like his tone. It was a little too authoritative for her, especially as he was speaking to her, in her home. "Do we?"

"Sit. Unless you want me to carry you?"

"No." She glared at him, and after a stubborn moment of glaring, and letting him know she wasn't going to be bossed around, she hopped to an armchair between the fire and tree. If she wasn't in a bad mood, she might have found the living room cozy and charming with the crackling fire and glowing Christmas tree.

Cade returned a few minutes later with coffee. "Let me know if you need more milk."

She glanced at the color. It looked perfect. She accepted the cup, murmured thanks. "I never made a fire in here," she added.

"Took me a bit to find a lighter or matches. Made me wonder how often you actually build a fire."

"Not often." *Not ever*, she silently corrected. "The basket of firewood is usually for show, but I have a ton of firewood on the side of the house."

"In that case, I'll restock your basket. Don't want to ruin your display."

She couldn't tell if he was joking or not. She studied his face, his strong features unsmiling, his strong jaw freshly shaven. "What time did you arrive this morning?" she asked.

"I slept here last night."

Her mouth opened, closed. She wasn't sure what to make of that. "I didn't know."

"I heard you moving around in the night. I wanted to check on you, but was afraid I'd scare you."

"I forgot water last night. Woke up needing medicine. Ended up drinking out of a faucet."

"Like a good cowgirl."

"I didn't think you liked the train room."

"It's better than the teddy bear room."

She made a face. "You are more grizzly than teddy."

"When do you usually like to eat?"

"I don't—"

"Great. I'll make us breakfast in a half hour." He left the

living room without waiting for a response, and MerriBee listened to his footsteps on the hall stairs.

His boots made a hard, thudding sound, very masculine, rather imposing, and she wasn't comfortable with it, or him. This was her home, her haven, and he was turning everything upside down, inside out. Yes, she was grateful, but she needed boundaries and right now she didn't know where they were.

She was in the kitchen when he returned, trying to make a cup of tea since the coffee hadn't agreed with the medicine she was taking. She was standing in the exact spot from a few days ago, when he'd come to tell her he wouldn't be staying. But this time he had no coat, hat, or duffel. He was just a man in a faded black thermal shirt, Wrangler jeans, boots, and belt.

But seeing him pause in the doorway was like déjà vu. She felt an intense rush of awareness, and again, a memory of another life, another man. John—but not John.

"After breakfast, I'll give you my credit card," Cade said. "We'll get things squared away so you don't have to worry about it later."

"The Bramble House should have a room for you—"

"I've canceled my reservation there. I'll be staying here."

"I haven't agreed."

"You're in no condition not to agree."

The truth annoyed her. He annoyed her. MerriBee pressed her lips together to hold back the things she wanted to say to him.

Instead, she counted to five. "How many nights do you intend to stay?" she asked, assuming her professional nurse voice, the one she used with her most challenging patients.

He glanced around the kitchen, his blue eyes narrowed as if not totally happy with what he was seeing, which just made her mad all over again. The kitchen was her favorite room in the house. It was white and cream with lovely marble counters and the most fantastic island. An antique sled hung over the island, the wooden sled filled with red and cream Christmas decorations. The wreaths on the window had cheerful red plaid ribbons. The antique china hutch on the far wall was filled with her favorite vintage Christmas dishes.

"Through Christmas," he said bluntly. "Unless Dot needs me back sooner."

It was none of her business but she couldn't help asking, "Who is Dot?"

"My boss."

Relief rushed through her, and the relief was so strong she felt annoyed with herself. She barely knew Cade. She shouldn't care who Dot was.

But apparently she did.

The sharp whistle of the teakettle pierced the air. Merri-Bee hopped forward on her crutches to turn the gas burner off, but Cade stepped between her and the stove. "I've got it," he said. "Please just go sit down."

"It's my house."

"Yes, but right now I'm your nurse—"

"Not my nurse. You're my lodger, my guest. I'm not paying you to be here."

"You're so prickly today."

"You don't like my house. You don't like my kitchen. You don't like me."

"You've got two of the three right. I don't like the house and the kitchen, but I do like you. I wouldn't be here otherwise." He opened a cupboard looking for mugs. Frowning, he pulled out two red glazed mugs with green Christmas trees. "Don't you have anything else to drink out of?"

"Those are Waechtersbach. They're collectibles."

"They hurt my eyes." Cade carried the mugs to the stove, glanced around the kitchen. "Where's the tea?"

"In those canisters. Each canister has a different variety."

"You mean, your reindeer?"

"Yes, it's a set. Dasher, Dancer, Prancer, Vixen—"

"Just having a cup of tea is a challenge around here," he muttered, cutting her off.

"I heard that."

He glanced over his shoulder, brow furrowed, blue gaze piercing. "Why are you still here? You're supposed to be sitting down, taking weight off your ankle. By the way, what kind of tea?"

MerriBee leaned on the crutches, feeling ill at ease in her

kitchen, as well as unusually aggravated, which was wasn't right as this bright sun-filled space was her favorite room in the house. "The huckleberry one if you can find it."

"Dot likes huckleberry tea, too."

"How many years have you worked for her?"

"Off and on since I was sixteen. Full-time since I was twenty-two, and finished serving in the army."

"You enlisted?" she asked.

"The moment I turned eighteen. Left the week of my high school graduation. Now sit somewhere so I can bring you your tea and start making breakfast."

CADE WATCHED HER hop into the dining room where she stood stork-like, on one foot while she awkwardly pulled out a chair with her good hand, and then sat down at the table, her long red hair still matted on the side with staples and stitches. If she were his, he'd wash her hair for her, and then comb it out so that it wouldn't tangle. But she wasn't his, and apparently she didn't have anyone, because last night when she'd been hurt, she called him.

And now she sat at the big table all by herself, looking a little lost, looking like a princess on her own.

He hadn't slept well last night, aware of her downstairs, aware that she was struggling. He'd wanted to help her, but it wasn't his job.

She wasn't his job.

But he wasn't going to just let her struggle.

She was young and pretty, and already a widow. He was very attracted to her and the attraction made him restless. Normally, this kind of attraction was handled by satisfying the itch. Get her naked, get her in bed, the itch would disappear. But he couldn't do that with her. She was off-limits physically, and not just because she'd lost a fight to her front steps, but she didn't need someone like him invading her space, complicating her life, and then bailing, because it's what he'd do. He bailed before attachments could be made, bailed without making commitments. He bailed on forever.

Cade had had his share of girlfriends, several that were long-term, including one that would have been a good Mrs. Hunt, if he'd been the marrying kind. But he wouldn't commit to Polly, and she'd gone on and married his best friend. Polly and Dean were expecting a baby now, and he was glad for her, glad for them. It seemed like everyone wanted a family but him.

Cade found a stack of red and green quilted place mats in a kitchen drawer and set two places on the dining table, his place setting across from hers.

He could feel her gaze as he arranged the silverware and then folded two paper towels for them to use as napkins.

"What brings you to Marietta?" she asked, when he returned with plates of eggs, bacon, and toast. "Are you meeting local ranchers?"

He could have lied to her, but after last night, he didn't

feel like playing games. There was no reason she couldn't know the truth. "I'm hoping to meet the Wyatts."

"You could have met Joe last night!"

He disappeared into the kitchen and returned with ketchup and hot sauce. "I don't know if he's the Wyatt I'm looking for," he said, sitting down at the table.

"I think there is only one Wyatt family here—they're a big family, and most live in Paradise Valley."

"The one I want to talk to has a place in Utah."

"Billy?" she said.

He liberally splashed hot sauce all over his eggs before pushing the condiments toward her. He was surprised how well she knew the Wyatts.

"But they all come home for Christmas," MerriBee added. "Sophie was just telling me about their Christmas plans last night."

He took a bite, and then another. "What are their plans?" he asked after cleaning half of his plate.

"They just like to be together at the ranch. They come together for their mom's sake, as well as their grandfather. Mr. Wyatt, the senior Mr. Wyatt, he's a love. Probably my favorite Wyatt."

"How have you gotten to know them all so well?"

"This last summer Sophie and I made jam together." She nodded at the dark berry jam he was spreading on his toast. "That's one of the ones we made."

He took a bite and nodded approvingly. "It's good."

"If you want to meet the Wyatts, I can arrange something—"

"No. I'll handle it my way." He finished his toast, wiped his hands on the paper towel. "I'll leave you alone so you can eat. Eggs are terrible cold." Cade carried his plate to the kitchen and after scraping his plate, he put it in the hot water to soak.

This was such a bad idea being here.

Nothing about it felt right. But leaving her felt wrong.

But maybe going out for a couple hours would help. Maybe creating some space for a bit would help the tension tying him in knots.

MERRIBEE WAS NOT someone who sat around and watched TV. She couldn't remember the last time she'd watched anything other than a half hour of the news, and even then, it'd been weeks since she'd done that. The news was never uplifting and the headlines increasingly dramatic, as well as polarizing, and she was just better off without that daily dose of negativity. However, with her left wrist in a thick cast, and her vision still a little blurry from that blow to her head, she wasn't good for wrapping, or knitting, or reading, and so after Cade left that morning to focus on his business, she settled on the couch, propping her ankle up and turning on the TV.

For nearly five minutes, she went through the guide, trying to find a show, but nothing appealed, not with her thoughts so scattered. She didn't know what to make of Cade. He was certainly protective, thoughtful, helpful, but there was also a tension between them that wasn't comfortable, an awareness that unsettled her. An awareness that made her aware of herself as a woman. Cade was reminding her that she wasn't just a nurse, or a worker bee, but a woman.

The next two days were more of the same. Breakfast prepared by Cade, and then he'd head out and do whatever it was he wanted to do, and then he'd return early afternoon and tackle small jobs around the house. MerriBee longed to wash her hair, but couldn't do that until Tuesday evening and even then she couldn't soak the stitches. It'd be just a quick shampoo and rinse, but it would be wonderful to finally get her hair clean.

She was going to need to enlist Cade's help, though and she thought the easiest place would be at the kitchen sink. She'd just tip her head over and using the faucet hose, she'd shampoo and rinse her hair upside down. When she told him her plan, he wasn't on board. "I'll drive you to a hair place. It'd be better if you were in a proper shampoo chair. They can keep the stitches from getting too wet."

"I don't want anyone to see me like this."

"What's wrong with you?"

"I look like I got in a fight."

"You did. With your front steps. It happens."

"Not to me."

"That's because you're a rookie. On the ranch, my hands get kicked and bucked all the time. Bruises and stitches become a badge of honor."

"Glad I don't have your job then."

"Just like I'm glad I don't have yours. But we do want to take care of you, and keep those stiches clean, so call around and find a place that can get you in and I'll take you whenever you're ready."

MerriBee thought it was no point telling him that she didn't have a stylist but when she did need a cut, she'd usually go to The Wright Salon, the pink hair salon owned by Amanda Wright, and the place Sophie Wyatt worked as a bookkeeper and sometimes front desk manager. MerriBee called the salon now, and it was Amanda who answered. Although the salon was closing soon, when Amanda heard what MerriBee needed, she told her to come down right away and she'd take care of her herself.

The salon was just two blocks over, and normally, it was somewhere MerriBee would walk, but with her sprained ankle and her difficulty walking with crutches due to her wrist, she let Cade drive her.

Amanda was wonderful, carefully shampooing Merri-Bee's hair, and giving her a lovely gentle scalp massage—away from the wound. She rinsed her hair clean, applied a conditioner everywhere but on her stitches and again rinsed, before helping her to her chair where she detangled the long strands, and blew dry her curls into soft waves that spilled down her back.

With the top layer of hair lightly combed over the stitches, the staples and threads were no longer visible. MerriBee smiled at her reflection. Except for the bruise on her cheekbone, she looked good as new.

"Now all pretty for your date night," Amanda said, taking the plastic cape off MerriBee's shoulders.

"With who?" MerriBee answered with a laugh.

Amanda nodded into the entrance where Cade filled up a lot of space. "He's a pretty good-looking cowboy."

MerriBee shook her head. "We're not dating. He's just renting a room from me."

Amanda gave her a look in the mirror. "He's in your house, and there's no romance? MerriBee, you might be an angel at the hospital, but you're still a woman. Live a little!" And then she thought of something. "Unless he's married?"

"No! He's single." MerriBee frowned. "At least, I think he's single."

After paying for her hair, MerriBee took Cade's arm, and leaned on him, as she hopped through the front door and out onto the salon's small porch. It had grown dark while she was inside, and the big trees in front of the house-turned-salon now glowed with pink lights.

"She likes pink doesn't she?" Cade said.

"So, which do you prefer? Her pink house, or my Christmas house?" she asked, hop-hopping down the walkway, but at such a slow pace, Cade sighed and picked her up.

"Hey," she protested. "I'm not nine." And truthfully, she didn't feel nine, not when Cade's face was just inches from hers, and his cool blue eyes made her feel breathless and warm. He *was* good-looking, and he was in her house, and when he held her close, she found it hard to think of anything else.

His cool gaze locked with hers a moment before he continued to the truck. "I'm very aware that you're not nine."

Something in his deep voice made her pulse quicken, and heat rushed through her, making her feel strangely weak. "Should we go home or go get food?" she asked, sliding back on the seat. "I mean, since we're out, and its dinnertime, should we go eat somewhere?"

"That's a good idea. I'm hungry."

"What do you want?" she asked, as he came around to the driver side.

"Anything."

"Then let's go to the Mexican restaurant on Main Street. Does that sound okay?"

"Do they have beer and chips and salsa?"

"Yes."

"Perfect."

Rosa's wasn't very busy and the smiling hostess told them to feel free and sit anywhere. MerriBee let Cade choose, and he selected a big corner booth in the front room. MerriBee slid into the booth and sighed with pleasure as she eased her coat off. The restaurant was warm and smelled of grilled onions and peppers, and fragrant with spices. "I haven't been here in ages," she said. "And my mouth is watering just sitting here."

"What do you usually order?"

"Fajitas at dinner. Their tostada salad at lunch."

The chips and salsa arrived immediately, and they ordered fajitas for two, with both beef and chicken, and then Cade's beer arrived, and he settled back with a contented sigh. "This was a good call," he said, lifting his bottle in a salute. "Thank you."

"You haven't eaten anything but chips yet."

"No, but it's a great atmosphere and a nice change from the house." He must have seen her mock outrage because he laughed and added, "Your house doesn't bother me as much as it used to. I've unplugged the tree in my room and that's made a difference."

"Why do you hate Christmas?"

"My—stepdad—found a way to ruin it every year, and after a while, I just wished November turned into January, and that the month of December wasn't part of the calendar."

"But what about the meaning of Christmas?" she asked carefully, not wanting to be preachy, but at the same time, curious. "That didn't matter, either?"

"You mean baby Jesus and all that?" Cade's upper lip curled. "There wasn't much faith in our family. You only heard God mentioned if Jimmy was cursing."

"Jimmy?"

"The stepdad." He hesitated. "But growing up, I thought he was my dad. I was eighteen when I found out he wasn't. It was a shock, but also a relief. I loved discovering I wasn't related to that guy."

"Your mom never told you?" MerriBee asked.

"No." He rubbed at a corner of the beer label, smoothing it where it had bubbled up. "I wish she had, though. Or at least left me something to help point me in the right direction."

"So, you have no idea?"

"I'm beginning to piece it together, but it's taken years. And I worry, by the time I find him, will he even be alive?"

"You're only thirty—"

"Thirty-two," he corrected.

"He's most likely in his fifties, maybe sixties, but, Cade, that's young. If he's healthy, he'd still be around."

Their dinner arrived, a large hot skillet with sizzling meat and vegetables, along with foil wrapped tortillas, cheese, sour cream and more salsa. They focused on their food and conversation shifted to dinners on the ranch, and how all the hands took turns cooking on the weekends, so the cook had weekends off.

MerriBee asked about the number of people who worked on the ranch and about Cade's job specifically. He told her that his favorite part of his job was being outside, in the saddle. He said he didn't think he'd ever had a good night's sleep until his first summer on the ranch. The ranch changed everything for him. Gave him purpose, as well as an identity.

"I've taken a DNA test," he said. "The test showed that I share the same DNA as Billy Wyatt."

"That was smart of you to take a DNA test."

"I didn't do it to find my birth father. I'd taken it to find my sister." His head lifted, his gaze meeting hers. "A sister I knew nothing about until I'd returned to Wyoming after serving in the army."

"So you didn't know about her until your twenties?"

He nodded. "Jimmy came to see me on the Sundowner Ranch. He'd been drinking and was in a foul mood. I remember thinking thank God this man isn't related to me. Thank God I don't have to deal with him daily, but then he told me that my mom had had an affair and gotten pregnant, and he was already raising one brat that wasn't his, but he wasn't going to raise another. So he told Mom to get rid of it. She went away, had the baby, gave it up for adoption, and then came home to us."

MerriBee felt sick. "You didn't know any of this?"

"No. I was thirteen at the time, in eighth grade, playing sports, trying to pass classes. Trying to survive at home." He drummed his fingers. "Jimmy said the baby was a girl. My sister would be nineteen now. I've been looking for her ever since Jimmy told me about her. I haven't found her yet. I took a DNA test four years ago, hoping it would provide some leads. Instead of finding her, the DNA test led me here to the Wyatts."

"Oh, Cade, I'm sorry."

"Don't be sorry. I'm going to be find her, and you have no idea what a relief it is not being Jimmy O'Connell's kid."

In bed that night, MerriBee kept thinking about her conversation with Cade, and his complicated history. She couldn't imagine growing up and thinking this was your family, these were your people, only to discover years later that much of it was a lie, and that the only sibling you had was somewhere out there, lost to you.

His story weighed on her. Cade had done so much for her. He'd gone out of his way for her again and again. She wanted to do something for him.

It took some thinking, but just as she fell asleep, an idea came to her. She'd make some calls tomorrow.

CHAPTER FIVE

A LIGHTBULB HAD burned out in the kitchen, spotlighting the sleigh hanging over the island. Cade couldn't figure out how MerriBee got the sleigh up there in the first place. She definitely had a little crazy in her, but he did, too, so maybe it was okay.

He should go, get out of the house, put space between them, but if he was honest, he didn't want to. He liked being near her. Liked to make her smile, liked that flash in her eyes when he teased her. She needed someone to make her smile, someone who'd help take care of her. It crossed his mind that he needed to be needed. It wasn't a hardship for him being here. It was a gift. He couldn't imagine being sent away from the Sundowner and wandering Paradise Valley on his own.

Everyone needed to be needed. Everyone needed to belong somewhere. And if he wasn't careful, he'd get too comfortable here, and never want to leave MerriBee.

Cade headed out then, killing time exploring the different communities tucked in the mountain ranges. He'd grown up with the Big Horn Mountains, and now he was getting to know the Gallatin Range and the Absarokas.

IT WAS MIDAFTERNOON when he returned to Marietta and discovered a big pickup parked outside the red gingerbread Christmas house. He wasn't sure if the truck belonged to someone down the street, or if MerriBee had a visitor. It was a newer truck, with heavy-duty snow tires, and a serious-looking hitch on the back, as if the truck was accustomed to pulling sizable trailers.

Stepping into the house, he took off his hat, and paused at the voices coming from the living room. MerriBee's and more. A woman and a man?

He walked through the foyer to the living room. The fire crackled. The tree lights shone in multicolor splendor, and MerriBee was sitting in her favorite chair between the fireplace and the tree, an ottoman propping up her ankle and a pillow tucked under her left elbow, keeping her wrist level. Her long hair was still glossy from her shampoo and blow-out. She'd put on some makeup, but enough for him to find her soft mouth even more enticing.

He'd spent the last four hours just driving to keep from thinking about her mouth, but it was impossible. He wanted to kiss her. But just kissing her wouldn't be enough. He knew that. And so he'd kept driving instead of returning to the house where he'd be alone with her.

As it turned out, he needn't have worried. She had

guests, and Cade forced his attention to the couple on the couch. From his profile, the man matched the truck—big, broad-shouldered, a cowboy hat on his lap. The woman at his side had a long brown braid, and she held his hand.

Conversation broke off as Cade entered the room. MerriBee smiled up at him, expression sunny. "Join us, Cade. I was hoping you'd return soon. These are my friends, Sam and Ivy Wyatt. They just dropped off twenty-four pounds of coffee from Bear Coffee for each of my Christmas baskets. Isn't that wonderful?"

It took him a moment to process what she'd said, not sure he'd heard correctly. Her friends, Sam and Ivy Wyatt. Did she say Wyatt?

But from that wide smile of hers, a wide delighted smile, he was sure her friends were Wyatts, and Cade would bet serious money that Wyatts hadn't ended up in her living room today, by chance.

Cade seethed inwardly. He hadn't wanted to be thrust at a Wyatt like this. He'd wanted to do more investigating on his own, ask more questions, and learn what he could without any of them knowing he was here asking questions about them.

Sam Wyatt had stood to greet him and Cade saw Sam's expression change, from a friendly welcoming to something less open.

His wife, tall and slender, had started to rise as well, but she sat back down, equally confused. She glanced from Cade to her husband, and then back again.

Cade understood the double takes. He was shocked as well. It wasn't quite like looking in the mirror, but his resemblance to Sam Wyatt was uncanny.

They had similar noses, mouths, and jaws. Similar foreheads with thick, straight eyebrows. Cade was more fair, his hair a lighter blond, his eyebrows slightly lighter, too. But they were almost the same height. They had a similar build.

For a moment, no one said anything and then Cade remembered his manners, closed the distance between them, and extended his hand to Sam. "Nice to meet you, Sam. Cade Hunt."

Sam's hand wrapped around his, grip firm. It was a long handshake. Sam searched Cade's eyes. "You remind me of someone," Sam said in a low voice. "I'm not sure what to say."

"Well, you and I might want to talk sometime," Cade said, feeling awkward, and caught off guard.

Cade liked control, and he was happiest in charge. He ran the Sundowner Ranch. He managed a dozen cowhands, a hundred horses, and two thousand cattle. He didn't like feeling exposed, or like an idiot, which was what he felt right now.

MerriBee was only just seeing the resemblance. Her lips parted and her eyes widened. "You look a lot alike. Maybe not twins, but brothers. Next thing you're going to tell me you're related." She laughed. No one else laughed. Her smile faded.

Silence filled the living room.

Cade could see a sheen of tears in MerriBee's eyes.

"Did I mess up?" she asked, her voice low. "If so, I'm sorry. I—"

"You didn't mess up," Cade said curtly, voice hard. "I've wanted to meet the Wyatt family. I'm in town to meet the family. And now I am."

Sam tapped his hat against his thigh. "You're here to meet us?"

Cade nodded slightly. "I was hoping to meet Billy, but apparently he lives in Utah now."

"He'll be here next week." Sam's narrowed gaze scrutinized Cade from head to toe. "What did you want to talk to him about?"

"It's complicated. But you might be able to answer some of my questions, too."

"Questions about the Wyatts?" Sam persisted.

Cade nodded again.

Sam exchanged a glance with Ivy before looking back at Cade. "We've a commitment this afternoon, but maybe in the morning? Would that work for you?"

"Schedule's wide open," Cade answered.

"How about coffee tomorrow morning? Eight at the Java Café?"

"I know where that is." Cade's gut felt hard and cold. His chest felt even tighter. He'd never met anyone that looked like him, and yet Sam did. He wasn't sure how he felt about that. He hadn't expected any of this to happen, least of all today. "I'll be there tomorrow."

"Cade manages the Sundowner Ranch," MerriBee interjected, looking a little less pleased with herself.

"The Warner place," Ivy Wyatt said, her long brown ponytail sliding over her slim shoulder. "In the Big Horn Mountains."

"That's it," Cade said. "I've been there about sixteen years now, minus the years I spent in the army."

"Nice piece of land," Sam added.

"Do you know it well?" Cade asked.

"It's not that far from here, not the way the crow flies," Sam answered.

"And we've spent a lot of years competing in Wyoming," Ivy added. "Which is why we have to go. I've a lesson in Bozeman at three. We should go now. I hate keeping Ashley waiting."

"Ashley?" MerriBee said brightening. "Ashley Howe?"

Ivy nodded.

MerriBee turned to Cade. "She's a high school girl, a barrel racer, in Bozeman and was paralyzed a couple years ago in an accident on their farm. Ivy has her riding again." She looked at Ivy. "Didn't she just compete for the first time again?"

"She did. I'm so proud of her."

"Well, go. I'd hate to make you wait."

Goodbyes were said and Cade walked the Wyatts to the door. But after he closed the door behind them, he stood in the hall and tried to gather his thoughts, and manage his emotions, because he wasn't happy with MerriBee. He wasn't happy at all.

❧

MERRIBEE HAD MESSED up. She knew it by Cade's silence. She knew by the uncomfortable tension building that Cade was upset with her. Knots formed in her stomach as Cade walked slowly back to the living room. It had been a long time since someone was upset with her. A long time since she'd let someone down.

"I'm sorry," she said quietly.

He wasn't looking at her. His gaze was on a spot on the floor, just before her ottoman.

"I noticed you still have the plastic tubs from the Stroll in your car," he said. "Why don't I take them out and put them away for you."

"There's no rush. They can stay there."

"I might as well unpack your car. I have nothing else to do. Where do the tubs go?"

She swallowed hard. "Into the garage, please," she said in a small voice. "Against the wall by the water heater. It's where they were before."

"Does the garage door open?"

"No. You'll have to carry them through the house."

He started to leave but she couldn't stand him going with things so uncomfortable between them. "Cade, wait."

He stopped walking but he didn't turn around.

A lump filled her throat. She was so disappointed in herself. "I should have minded my own business. I made a mistake, and I'm really sorry, Cade." She swallowed hard. "As you know, I like to help. But sometimes I help too much."

"You're fine," he said flatly.

"No, I'm not, because you're not fine," she said, still talking to his back. "I overstepped, and I won't do it again, not with you."

He finally glanced at her, his jaw was still set, but his blue gaze wasn't as icy cold as she'd imagined. "Let it go," he said. "I was caught off guard, but everything's okay. Things always have a way of working out."

"Do you really believe that?" she asked, hopefully.

"It's what Dot says, and she's usually right about things."

"I promise to mind my own business in the future."

He smiled crookedly. "Not a bad idea, but I won't hold you to it."

MerriBee didn't know why her eyes were tearing up but she had to reach up and wipe the moisture from the corner of her eyes. "What does that mean?"

"It means that I know you need to help. Curbing your helpful nature might prove impossible."

He left for the kitchen where she heard him pick up her

keys from the mail cubby, and then head outside to begin bringing the tubs in. She exhaled, her heart feeling tender. She didn't like making people unhappy.

MerriBee glanced around the cheerful living room with the many Christmas decorations.

For the first time since putting everything up this year, she wasn't sure she liked it. It was an awful lot of festivity. Was it maybe too much?

Was she doing too much, trying too hard?

She decorated every year for John. It was her way of honoring his memory. He'd loved Christmas and she'd been determined to keep his spirit alive by putting up the trees, hanging the wreaths, wrapping garland around the banisters. She put out the candles, and angels, the nativity set for him. She didn't need it for her. She wasn't even sure how she felt about Christmas anymore. Christmas had become an awful lot of work. Somehow, she'd become so busy with doing and giving she'd gone a bit numb.

Maybe it was time to cut back. Fewer trees. Fewer decorations. Less fuss. Less needing to help—

She broke off, grimaced. Cade was right. That last one would be difficult to change.

CADE UNPACKED MERRIBEE'S car, carrying the half dozen oversized tubs to her front step, and then through the house to the garage door, making a mental note to check out the garage door and see why it didn't work. In a place like Marietta, she should park her car in her garage, keep it out of the elements. But it wasn't until he opened the hall door leading into to the garage and turned on the garage light that he saw why she couldn't park in there—beyond the whole nonworking garage door thing.

Her garage was like Santa's workshop. There were rows and rows of tables, and each of the tables were covered with large wicker baskets. They were half full, too, with boxes of items on the cement floor between the rows of tables. The Christmas baskets. The result of all her fundraising.

He carried the tubs to the far wall, stacking them in the empty space near the water heater, and then crossed to one of the tables to inspect a basket. It had some crinkle paper on the bottom with a variety of canned foods on top, plus a jar of her homemade jam. There were also small packages of festive holiday candy, several gift cards, a box of beautifully wrapped chocolates from Copper Mountain Chocolates. A tag was attached to the basket handle. He flipped it over to read the note. THE JOHNSONS: JAMES 37, JUSTINE 31, JR 7, JENNY 5, JOJO 3, AND JOHN JOHN 1.

He looked at the next basket and read the next tag—THE DAVIS FAMILY: ED 48, NANCY, 41, TIM 15, ABIGAIL 10.

Cade walked up and down the rows reading the names, noting the ones where there was no dad, or the basket where there seemed to be just grandparents and young children. One family had seven kids. Another family had just lost their baby and she wanted to do something special for them.

These people were not strangers to her. She wasn't just organizing a holiday dinner for them, either. She was creating a personalized basket for every family. She cared about each of them, and from the gift cards tucked in with the sweets and treats, he could see she was trying to give something—even if it was just a little something—to everyone. On the table in front of the baskets she had notes, reminders of what she still needed to buy, dates she was supposed to pick up the turkey, ham, rolls, and pies.

He felt a tug of emotion. He'd never met anyone like MerriBee before. He didn't know what to do with her, either. If only he could just take her to bed, make love to her, make them both feel good. Sex would release some of the tension he felt. It would also simplify things. He liked things simple. Uncomplicated.

If only MerriBee wasn't so complicated.

If only she wasn't intent on saving the world.

If only she had others looking out for her, taking care of her. Because from what he'd seen so far, MerriBee was very much on her own.

Cade left the garage, turned off the light, and closed the door, but the dozens of half-filled Christmas baskets remained with him.

CADE HAD OFFERED to make dinner but MerriBee felt guilty

having him work so much, while a guest in her home. "What about pizza?" she suggested.

"Sure. I can order."

"I'll do it. Just tell me what you like."

"All kinds. Surprise, me," he answered, and since that was all he'd said, she ordered two medium pizzas—a classic pepperoni, and her personal fave, Canadian bacon, pineapple and extra cheese—along with a house chopped salad.

She'd prepaid for the pizzas so when they arrived Cade carried them to the living room, and brought out plates and napkins. He asked if she'd minded if he turned on the news while they ate. She didn't.

MerriBee was happy just to relax. She was also grateful Cade didn't seem to hold a grudge or stay angry about her interference earlier in the day.

Cade was relatively quiet, but also, good company. He could see what needed to be done, and he just did those things, whether it was unload the dishwasher or change a lightbulb or salt the sidewalk.

After the news program he'd wanted to watch ended, he muted the TV and rose to collect their plates.

"Cade, you don't have to wait on me. I can manage, you know."

"I can't just sit around," he answered. "I need stuff to do."

"I could teach you how to knit," she offered.

"I have a feeling you're only half-teasing," he said, putting the plates on the boxes and carrying all into the kitchen.

"You're not wrong," she called to him. He didn't answer but maybe he hadn't heard her. He was running the water, rinsing—or washing—the plates. The man was certainly tidy.

He returned a few minutes later with a cup of coffee. "I've put the kettle on, in case you want tea."

"I'm fine right now," she said. "But thank you."

He was back a minute later but he didn't sit. He added a log to the fire he kept perpetually burning, and then poked at the embers. "I don't know how you take a month off without losing your mind. I haven't even been away from the ranch for a week and I'm already going nuts."

"You can't go back?"

"Not until after Christmas. Dot asked me to disappear while her family is there this year. Last year I butted heads with her great-nephew, and he complained about me to her."

"Why were you butting heads?"

"He—and his family—take advantage of Dot's generosity. I find it incredibly disrespectful."

"Do you tell him this?"

"No. But I'm not going to let Alistair railroad her. I'm not going to let anyone take advantage of her."

MerriBee adjusted the pillow under her cast. "Do they do that?"

He straightened and turned to face her. "They know the ranch will one day be theirs, and I don't mind helping them out, and am always happy to lead a ride, do an airport run, or harness horses to the sleigh, but I don't work for them. I work for Dot." Cade hesitated then smiled. "And yes, I do tell him that."

MerriBee smiled back. "I wondered."

"The first time they came out I had no expectations. They were city people, visiting a ranch in winter. Of course, everything would be new. But it's been five or six years now, and each visit is the same. They're helpless. They expect to be waited on. But the Sundowner is a real working ranch. I think it's time they learned to saddle their own horses, and after a ride, brush down the horses. If they want to inherit the ranch, they need to learn to care for it. They also need to care for her."

"Dot?"

He nodded. "It's time they helped with Christmas, time they asked what they could do for her, instead of expecting her to organize their Christmas holidays every year."

"Do they?"

"Yes. The entitlement is galling." His voice hardened. "But I've never said that to her, nor would I. It's not my place. They are her family, and they will be the future owners, but Dot is special, and if they'd only get off their phones and iPads and computers, they'd discover she's a fascinating woman, with an amazing past. When her brothers all died, she took on that ranch, and ran it when women didn't do things like that. She has stories and so much wisdom to share."

"She's lucky to have you in her corner."

"I'm the lucky one."

"And you don't like to leave her."

"Anything could happen."

"But I bet it won't."

CADE HAD A hard time falling asleep and staying asleep that night. There was so much on his mind, so much tangling his thoughts. He'd gone to the garage earlier to use the stepladder to change a lightbulb, and he'd paused to study the baskets again, and read some more of her notes. Pick up hams… get turkeys… confirm the pies with the diner the day before…

He had no idea how she did it all.

He wasn't sure why she needed to do it all.

Tomorrow morning, he'd meet with Sam, and hopefully Sam could get Cade in touch with his biological dad. After all these years of not knowing who his real dad was, it'd be a relief to have answers.

Maybe meet the man who'd made him.

The issue of paternity shouldn't matter as much as it did, but it kept Cade awake much of the night. Perhaps if Jimmy had been a better man, Cade wouldn't feel such a burning need to know where he came from, but Jimmy hadn't been a good man, and Cade wanted to meet someone, somewhere he was related to. Someone that maybe would be his family.

Cade gave up trying to sleep at four thirty, and after going downstairs to make coffee, he carried a big cup upstairs to the turret morning room to text with the staff on the ranch, make sure everything was running smoothly, and when the horizon lightened, watch the sun rise.

Whether in Marietta, or in Wyoming, Cade started every day virtually the same way—up early, have coffee, and watch the sun rise. There was something powerful in watching light chase away darkness, as the rising sun warmed the cool dawn.

MerriBee was hovering near the front door when he came down the stairs at seven thirty. "What are you doing?" he asked, seeing her just standing in the hall, leaning against a crutch.

"I wanted to say good luck." She looked nervous… for him. "I hope it will go well."

"There's no reason to be worried. Everything will be fine."

"Cade?"

"Hmm?"

"Why are you interested in them?"

The corner of his mouth lifted. "You can't help yourself, can you?"

"Do you think you might be related to all of them? You'd have to be, wouldn't you?"

He shrugged. "I don't know yet."

It took a good couple of minutes for Cade's old truck to warm up, and then another couple of minutes to drive downtown and park on Main Street. He was early at the Java Café, but figured he'd find a table and maybe order something before they got there. Only it didn't quite work out that way. Sam Wyatt was already there, and he wasn't alone. He'd brought his older brother, Joe, and they'd already ordered coffee.

Cade suddenly didn't want anything and after the introductions, he pulled out a chair at the table and sat down. Joe and Sam sat down again, too. They were three big men at one small, antique card table and there wasn't a lot of space. For a moment no one said anything and then Cade forced himself to speak.

"I'm not sure where to begin," he said. "I was raised in Sheridan, Wyoming. My mom died when I was eighteen. It was after her death that the man I thought was my dad, told me he wasn't. Furthermore, I had a half-sister, too, a baby my mom gave up for adoption when I was thirteen." He paused, considered his words. "At first I didn't believe him. I thought he was just being mean, because that's who Jimmy was. A bully. He needed to feel powerful. But a couple months later, when I enlisted, I had to track down a copy of my birth certificate, and low and behold, there was no James O'Connell on the certificate. There was no father's name. Apparently when I was two or three Jimmy adopted me, which is how I became Cade O'Connell, but after learning that James was not my biological dad, I changed my name back to Hunt, my mom's maiden name, and that's who I've been ever since."

Sam and Joe said nothing. They just looked at him, and yet it was strange sitting at the same table, strange because beyond the resemblance to each other, there was also that resemblance to *him*. It wasn't just looks, too, but in mannerisms, and Sam particularly. From the way he sat, moved, the narrowing of his eyes—it was very much like Cade. Sam wasn't a mirror, but he was close enough. They clearly shared the same DNA.

DNA. That's what had brought him here. That's what this was all about.

"I spent years trying to find my sister, years trying to figure out who my father was, since it wasn't Jimmy, but there were no leads, not until a few months ago when a DNA test I'd taken years ago matched me with someone. And that someone was your brother Billy." Cade stopped talking. The silence was heavy, which was a stark contrast to the noisy café, and the long line at the counter.

Joe shifted in his chair. "I don't know anything about DNA tests. I've never had one done." He looked at his brother. "Billy did though, didn't he? When he was establishing paternity."

Sam nodded. "But why would that be up on a website?"

"It's one of those places people go to trace their family tree, and your brother's information was part of a family tree," Cade answered. "The tree is private, but because of the DNA, it linked him to me. According to the DNA strands, William was a fairly close relation, either an uncle, a nephew, or a first cousin."

"Not a brother?" Sam asked.

Cade shook his head. Was that what they were thinking? Was that why Sam had brought Joe today? "No, we would have needed to share more DNA for that, and we don't."

For a moment there was just silence at the table, and then Joe shifted in his chair, broad shoulders squaring. "There's no William in our family, just Billy. That's what he's always been called." Joe's words were blunt. "So, if through DNA you are related to Billy, you're also related to us." Silence stretched again for a moment, and then a faint smile curved Joe's lips. "Not sure if I should congratulate you, or offer condolences."

For the first time since sitting down at the table, some of the tension knotting Cade's shoulders eased. At least Joe Wyatt had a sense of humor. Humor was essential at this point. "So no one else in your family has taken a DNA test?"

"Not that I know of." Sam glanced at Joe. "Did you?"

Joe shook his head. "It's never crossed my mind that I should. But maybe I need to."

"Can you show me how this DNA site works?" Sam asked.

"It's easier on the computer, but I printed out some pages that show the information the website gave me, revealing how William and I are linked. Your brother and I have been connected, but so far, that's the only close family member there is."

"Who are those people?" Sam asked, pointing to information further down.

"Fourth and fifth cousins it says," Cade answered. "But there's no one I know."

Sam scanned the page and shook his head. "No one I know, either."

"But if Billy is my cousin, then he—and you all—would know my dad." Cade hesitated, then added, "Not that I'm trying to claim any family connection. I'm just trying to find out who my real dad was and if he'd be open to meeting me."

His words, *my real dad*, seemed to hang in the air, and Sam and Joe exchanged glances again.

"Granddad," Sam said quietly. "He'd find all this very interesting."

"Mmm," Joe agreed, expression growing somber, his gaze now riveted to Cade's face. "It would be a shock."

"Too much of one?" Sam asked.

Joe continued to scrutinize Cade. "Not necessarily."

Cade didn't know their grandfather and couldn't add anything to the conversation. He knew so little about the Wyatts and hadn't gotten to reading up on Melvin Wyatt. "I don't know as much about your family as I'd like. It's been busy on the ranch, and quite frankly, research frustrates me.

I'm not as good with technology as I should be. I had some vacation time so I thought it made more sense to come here in person, and talk to Billy, and find out what I could, but I understand Billy's not here for another week.

"He and Tommy are both still in Las Vegas," Joe said.

"Competing in the NFRs," Cade said. "A bartender at the steak house told me. You're all professional rodeo cowboys."

"Were," Joe corrected. "I'm not anymore."

Sam gave his brother a side glance. "That's because Joe left the circuit to work the ranch with Granddad."

"Our dad was a rodeo cowboy," Joe said, ignoring the last bit. "As well as Uncle Samuel."

Cade felt a prickling at his name. Samuel. Was that his dad's name? "Sounds like it runs in the blood," he said quietly.

"You've never competed?" Sam asked him.

Cade shook his head. "Didn't even ride a horse until I was sixteen, but once I did, I knew where I belonged. Except for my four years of active duty, I've been on the Sundowner Ranch ever since."

For a moment no one said anything, and then Sam cleared his throat. "Here's what I know, if you're Billy's first cousin, that means you're our first cousin, and Granddad only had two kids, two sons. Our dad, and then our uncle Sam, who might be your dad."

Cade tried to keep his emotions in check. *His* dad. Not

Jimmy O'Connell. But Samuel Wyatt. It was heady stuff. "Can we ask your uncle to take a DNA test? Do you think he'd be willing?"

Neither of the Wyatts were in a hurry to answer. Joe finally did. "Samuel's gone. He died with our dad, in a car accident, on the way to a rodeo in Cheyenne."

Cade felt the words as if they were a blow.

His body sagged, and he drew a deep breath. He hadn't realized how much he'd wanted to meet his biological father until now. But there would be no meeting. No bond. No father-son relationship. The disappointment was heavy, almost suffocating. All this time he'd been pretending he didn't care, but obviously he did care. A great deal.

And to think his dad had died in Wyoming.

"What year was that?" he asked, when he could comfortably speak.

Joe named a year and Cade shook his head. It was possible that Samuel had fathered a baby. But if he had, did he know he'd gotten a girl pregnant? Had his mom ever told his dad?

Now, with both gone, Cade doubted he'd ever know.

"That must have been hard for your grandfather to lose both of his sons together like that," Cade said.

Joe shifted in his chair. "Raising us gave Granddad a purpose."

"Were you all living with him already?" Cade asked.

"We were in California," Sam said. "Just outside Sacramento. But Granddad sent Mom money to bring us all here. I was five when Dad died and we moved. I don't remember ever living in California. I don't remember much of Dad, either. But photos help. When I see photos of him, or our family, I can picture some things, but it's been too long."

"Cade, how old would you have been when Samuel died?" Joe asked.

"Almost five."

"Same age as me," Sam said.

Cade swallowed, glanced away, gaze fixed on the street beyond the coffee shop window. He hadn't expected to feel this conflicted. He'd wanted to know the facts but hadn't expected so much emotion.

"If you're Samuel's son, Granddad is going to want to meet you," Sam added.

"*If*," Joe repeated, emphasizing the word.

"Just look at him," Sam said under his breath. "He's family."

But Cade knew he wasn't their family. *They* were a family. The Wyatts were a family. He was a Hunt-O'Connell-Hunt. A dog-pound mutt. The Wyatts had strong bonds. They'd grown up on a piece of land that had been in the family for generations. They knew who they were, and where they belonged. Cade had never had that, not even as a kid.

"He does look like Uncle Sam," Joe agreed, "but I think we all need to take a DNA test. Granddad should, too."

"Granddad's not going to take a test without wanting to

know why—"

"And if he knows why, he's just going to want to meet Cade," Joe finished.

"So where does that leave us? What can we do?" Cade said, trying to manage his impatience.

"I think the three of us should take a DNA test at the same time," Joe said. "We should get the results back at the same time, and we then compare tests."

Cade clamped his jaw. He wasn't lying. He wouldn't make something like this up. But at the same time he understood their reservations. If he were in their shoes, he'd be the same. "I'll do whatever you want done."

"There's a facility in Bozeman that does DNA tests," Sam said. "Billy used it when he was establishing paternity for Beck. We can go there. Not sure if they can rush the results, but we can ask."

"When?" Joe asked.

"How about next Tuesday? Ivy and I are going to look at a horse in Idaho this weekend, but we'll be back Monday night."

"That works for me," Joe said.

Tuesday struck Cade as too long, but he didn't want to make waves. "For me as well."

"Not sure if we will need appointments," Sam said. "I'll make some calls and let you know what I find out."

Joe and Sam rose, shook Cade's hand, and headed out of the café. He hated the pang he felt as they walked together, talking. Growing up, he'd hated being an only child. He'd always wanted a brother.

Cade went to the counter, ordered coffee and breakfast, and while he waited for his number to be called, he thought about Sam and Joe, and the conversation. Cade was getting closer to the truth, and this was what he needed. For years, he'd wanted answers, and in less than a week he'd have something definitive, something that would also answer some of the questions Sam and Joe had.

Those answers would be a relief, but they'd also create new questions. Like how did his mom and biological dad meet? Were they just a random hookup? Had either of them cared about the other? And why didn't his mom tell his biological dad she was pregnant?

Did she not know how to find him?

Did she tell him and he didn't care?

Fear wasn't part of his vocabulary. Bears didn't scare him. Mountain lions didn't scare him. Intruders didn't scare him. Breaking wild horses didn't scare him either. But finding out who his dad was? Finding out where he came from? That was hard and proving to be a little bit terrifying.

Breakfast over, he carried his dishes to the bin and then headed out to his truck. The sky was clear, the sun bright, and a strong wind had cleared away the clouds. The day loomed before him. There were too many hours in the day for him right now, too much time on his hands. If he returned to MerriBee's, he'd be alone with her and thinking thoughts that weren't helpful, and he wasn't in the mood to fight temptation. In his current mood, he might just give in to it.

No, he had to get away, do something.

Lately all he did was drive and drive.

He was so tempted to just drive back to the ranch. It'd only be four and a half hours away. He could go, check up on everything, and be back in Marietta for dinner.

But Dot wouldn't like it.

Alistair wouldn't like it, either. That made Cade smile. But making Alistair miserable wasn't worth earning Dot's disapproval.

Maybe he couldn't show up today, but that didn't mean he couldn't check in again with Willis. In the truck, with the engine on and the heater warming the interior, Cade called his assistant foreman. "How are things?" Cade asked when Willis picked up.

"Nothing's changed from yesterday."

"Just answer my question."

"Things are fine, Cade. You need to relax."

Cade heard a dog bark, but not the ranch dogs. This was a shrill *yap-yap-yap*. "Where are you?"

"In the house. Just helped Emma clear the table."

"They still can't carry their dishes to the kitchen?"

"I think it's just a habit now."

The yapping grew louder. There sounded like two dogs now. "Why am I hearing barking?"

"Alistair's daughters brought their dogs. They're just little lap dogs but they're excited and running around the dining room."

"Did Dot know they were bringing dogs?"

"No. But what was she going to do once they were here?"

"Keep them contained. Not let them have free run of the house."

"I think they're supposed to be kept in the girls' rooms—"

"Which girls?"

"London and Paris."

"Those are not little girls. They're in their twenties!"

"I never said they were little girls. The dogs are little. But London and Paris didn't want to leave them behind. Apparently, the dogs have separation anxiety."

"The dogs managed to survive last year."

"But one of them didn't eat. London said it was too stressful."

"Then maybe London needs to stay home with her dog because the Sundowner is Dot's home and having little dogs running wild could get Dot hurt."

Willis sighed. "She's not hurt, though. She's fine. The staff is just worn out, and it's only been a week."

Cade held his breath, trying to gain control of his temper. The ranch was his home, and his refuge, and it had been since that first summer he worked there. Those summers during high school were the only thing that got him through the rest of the year. It had saved him, the peace he found on the ranch, as well as the sense of belonging. There was no peace at home. His parents fought constantly, his dad hurling insults at his mom. *Whore. Slut. Lazy. Useless.* He stayed out of the fights as long as his dad didn't lift his hand against his mom, but the moment his dad got physical, Cade stepped in.

Cade had ended up with bruises more than once to keep his dad from touching his mom, but Cade was young and strong. He could handle the fists and blows. His mom... no. Something was wrong with his mom. He didn't know what it was, only she hadn't been herself for a couple of years, and she seemed to be disappearing in front of him, sinking physically and emotionally into a very dark place.

"Can't wait for them to leave so I can return," Cade said.

"You and me," Willis answered, before speaking to someone in the same room. "Hey, Cade?"

"Yes?"

"Dot's here. She wants to talk to you."

Cade growled back in his throat and waited for her to come on the line.

"Cade," Dot said after a few moments, her voice still low and husky, but now with the quiver of age. "Didn't you just call yesterday?"

Some of his tension eased at hearing her familiar voice. "Yes, ma'am."

"Not your ma'am. I'm Dot, and I thought you were on vacation?"

"I'm trying."

"Not very hard," she said. She started to speak but her

115

voice was drowned out by barking dogs. Someone in the background was apparently speaking to the dogs but the dogs didn't seem to be listening.

"Sorry about that," Dot said when she could be heard again. "It's a houseful this year. Can't imagine the chaos when they start bringing babies."

"But you like it," he said, testing her, wondering if she'd tell him the truth.

"It's only for a few weeks once a year, and the twins are inordinately attached to their dogs. The girls dress them up in clothes. They travel in their purses. It's painful for them to be parted."

"Do the *girls* have jobs yet? They're twenty-six now."

"One does some marketing, the other is an influencer. Not sure what that means, but she has a lot of followers, quarter of a million, or something like that." She hesitated. "That is apparently a big deal."

HE RUBBED THE bridge of his nose, pained by the very sound of the word influencer. "Glad I'm not there."

"You'd lose your mind," Dot agreed, a smile in her voice. "The dogs even come to the dinner table. They sit on the girls' laps."

"*Dot.*"

"They're their babies."

"Maybe I should pop in, calm the chaos, remind the

Jameses of the rules."

"Now, Cade, are you saying I can't handle my own family?"

He closed his eyes, pictured her intelligent gaze, and her cloud of white hair that she braided every day and pinned in a bun at the back of her head. "No."

"If I weren't okay, you'd be the first person I'd call. I promise."

"Dot."

"Yes, Cade?"

"You're my only real family."

She was quiet a moment and then she said gently, "I know, my boy. You've always had my best interests at heart. Everything's fine here. My family has settled in and they're enjoying the snow. They've gone shopping and sledding and today Willis is taking them out in the sleigh. We're having a nice visit—even with the little dogs. There's no need to worry so much."

They said goodbye and hung up, but as Cade put his phone down on the leather bench seat, he felt as if a Clydesdale had just trotted across his chest.

He didn't know how not to worry about her. He'd spent the past ten years keeping an eye on Dot. Ten years dedicated to keeping her happy, comfortable, and safe. But if she didn't need him anymore, where did that leave him?

And if Alistair took over the ranch and wanted Cade gone, where would he go?

CHAPTER SIX

T HE DAY FELT endless. Cade had left early for his morning meeting at Java Café and he never came back. She'd waited for him, keeping an eye on the clock, but after a couple of hours, she realized he wasn't returning anytime soon and she needed to find something to do besides watch the clock.

MerriBee had never mastered the art of relaxation, and after days of accomplishing very little, she needed to get back on task. With her current limitations, she couldn't bake one-handed, and she couldn't drive or run errands, but she could tackle more wrapping. The cast was on her left hand, not her right. She could hold the paper down with the cast, and cut and tape with her right.

It took a few not so pretty attempts to figure out how to move things around and get an efficient assembly line going. She played Christmas carols as she wrapped, a mix of country and the old school crooners. It felt good to be doing something again, something productive. Having Cade in the house had done something to her resolve, impacted her discipline. Instead of feeling strong and independent, her thoughts would drift and she'd think about him, remembering something he'd said or done. She'd picture his face, his flannel shirts, his long legs, his boots. She kept wondering all day where he was and when he'd be back.

It was annoying fixating on him. She hadn't felt this way about anyone since... since... she stopped herself, not allowing herself to go there.

She wasn't going to compare Cade to John. That was ridiculous. There was no comparison. There never would be.

Irritated, MerriBee tore off a piece of tape—an overly long strip—and pressed it to the seam of red foil paper. It went on crooked. She glared at the creased paper. It was a messy job. She didn't like it. She could do so much better.

She was tempted to peel the tape off the back and try again, but it could also be covered with a ribbon. A wide ribbon would hide the ugly seam.

Her hand shook ever so slightly as she ran her fingertip under the tape, lifting it off. She carefully realigned the edges of the paper, carefully pressed the tape down again. Better.

She hadn't always been such a perfectionist. She hadn't always needed to stay constantly busy. She'd changed after John died.

When they first dated, he hadn't been ill, at least, she hadn't known he'd had cancer and was in remission. He told her after they'd been seeing each other for a few months, but since he was in remission, and he had good doctors, she hadn't worried much, because he'd told her he wasn't worried. He'd told her everything would be fine, and she believed him.

They became serious, so serious she was thinking he'd propose as they discussed the future, and the future they wanted together, but then one April, a week before Easter, he ended things with her, saying he needed to take care of some personal things, and he'd be returning to Colorado.

It had been a terrible breakup. She hadn't understood, couldn't understand. John, who'd been so open and so warm, cut off all communication. And then one day he was a patient on her floor. She was still new in oncology, and she read his chart, heart racing, horrified to discover that his bone cancer had spread to the point that there was nothing anyone could do, no more treatments to try. He was in the hospital because his body was shutting down. They'd been brought back together for her to say goodbye.

MerriBee was livid. She wasn't having any of it. She wasn't going to let him die. She forced more calories into him, upped his liquids, and between taking care of him physically, she demanded answers. Why hadn't he told her about his cancer? Did he break up with her because the cancer had returned with a vengeance?

John apologized, saying he was just trying to protect her. He said he couldn't burden her, that he wouldn't burden her, not after learning that his time was running out. She said she'd thought he loved her. John said he did. "Then if you love me," she said, ",marry me. Make me yours."

They were married in the hospital, but then he improved, so much so, that John was able to leave the hospital and he moved home with her, and for eleven months they had the most beautiful life together.

MerriBee reached for another gift box, and once again braced the red foil wrapping paper, unrolling it just enough.

Had she hoped that there would be a miracle? Had she believed God would save him?

After all, Jesus had saved Lazarus. Miracles existed. Miracles were all around them. She'd had faith. She believed. She believed with all of her heart, too.

But it hadn't been enough.

In the months after John was first gone, she couldn't think about God, couldn't allow herself to feel because she'd become angry. She'd felt betrayed. All those bible verses, all those scriptures. If you have faith like a grain of mustard seed...

MerriBee pressed her lips together, a lump filling her throat.

She'd had such faith. She'd believed she could move mountains.

She couldn't.

Five years later, her faith was different. It was quieter, less urgent, less fierce. Resigned, might be the best word. Resigned to help as best as she could, knowing her faith wouldn't save anyone, that her convictions were just that.

After he died, members from her church tried to set her

up. Three years after his death, she accepted her first date. He wasn't John. He wasn't anyone special. She went on a second date because he was kind, and a doctor, and they had medicine in common, but after a few more dates, she told him she wasn't ready. He was nice about it. She was just relieved to stop going through the motions, because she wasn't open to loving anyone else. She didn't want to find a person.

Another year passed, and she met another man, this time at the grocery store. He was new in town, and he asked her about her basket of hams—she'd just picked them up for her holiday baskets. She told him about the meals she organized. He insisted on paying for the hams, and then gave her another five hundred to cover incidentals. She thanked him, and they exchanged numbers. After the holidays, he asked her out. They went on a date. The date was fine—it had actually been fun—but then he'd kissed her, and he'd wanted her to come back to his place, and she'd frozen up. He wasn't John. He didn't kiss like John. She didn't want to be with him.

MerriBee knew John wouldn't have wanted her to stop dating and living, but with John gone, she didn't want to remarry. She loved being Merri Bradley, or Mrs. Bradley. She loved her memories of him, and was determined to keep those memories alive... forever. Or, as long as she could.

Five years ago, she'd made the decision she'd never re-marry, and because of that, she'd never have children.

Instead, she'd pour herself into her work, taking care of others. She had a vocation now, a true vocation, and she was committed to it.

Happy with it.

Most of the time.

A rap sounded on the door of her room. "MerriBee?"

Her heart jumped. Cade. Finally. "Come in," she said, blowing a tendril of hair from her eyes. "Door's unlocked."

"You're dressed?"

She laughed. "*Yes.*"

The door opened and he stood there, filling her doorway with shoulders too broad, and legs too long. He was wearing his customary uniform of boots, jeans, and a thick flannel shirt, and he had a faint mark on his forehead made by his cowboy hat. "Have you been with Sam Wyatt this whole time?" she asked, noting the fading light.

"No. Had coffee with Sam and Joe, and then I went for a drive."

"Joe was there, too?" she asked.

"Yes. Got to talk to both."

"Did they invite you back to their ranch?"

"No. Just drove around, explored the valley, had lunch in Emigrant, and then on the way back drove to the park on Copper Mountain, watched the ice-skaters on Miracle Lake."

She hopped back and sat down on the edge of the bed. "I love the lake in winter. So pretty. Were there a lot of skaters out today?"

"It wasn't very crowded. But it looked like some kids were arriving to practice hockey."

She tried pushing the same stubborn curl from her eyes but it refused to stay tucked behind her ear. "They've built a rink at the edge of town, but in winter the kids like to be out of doors," she said.

"I don't blame them. It looked like fun."

"Do you skate?" she asked him.

He shook his head. "Never had the time. How about you?"

"Yes, and ski, although I haven't done that in a number of years—" She broke off, because it crossed her mind that she hadn't done anything but work these past five years. No skating, skiing, rock climbing. No hiking or swimming. Her world had narrowed to such an extent that she'd shut out virtually everyone and everything.

He studied her a moment as if she was a puzzle he couldn't figure out. "I'm going to make stir-fry," he said. "I've never heard a single complaint, either, and I cook for a lot of guys on the ranch. *Hungry* guys, who don't like vegetables."

"Are you saying your stir-fry has no vegetables?"

"My stir-fry is full of vegetables, and they are delicious."

"You are already doing so much for me."

"You're not the only one who needs to stay busy. I need to work. Don't deprive me of an evening chore."

She heard the teasing note in his voice and it made her

feel warm on the inside, warm in a way that she hadn't felt since John died. "I'd hate to deprive you of your chores," she answered with mock seriousness.

"So you wrap and I'll cook, and I'll let you know when it's time to eat."

"Sounds like a plan."

Forty-five minutes later, Cade appeared at the door of her wrapping room to let her know that dinner was ready. Instead of eating at the dining room table, he'd arranged for them to eat in the living room, and he'd put together a little TV tray for her in front of her favorite chair, so she could eat more easily on her lap.

"Where did you get this from?" she asked, as he settled the wide wooden tray over her lap, the edges resting perfectly on the arms of the wingchair.

"I made it."

"*You* did? When?"

"Today, when I got home." He must have seen her incredulous expression because he snorted. "MerriBee, it's not art. It's a couple pieces of wood with a couple of nails."

"But it's so smooth."

"That's called sandpaper," he said, placing one of her Christmas place mats on the tray, and then setting it with the silverware. "It does impressive things."

She rolled her eyes even as heat crept up her cheeks. He'd made her a dinner tray. And maybe he was just being practical, but his thoughtfulness touched her. No one had ever made her anything before. "Still, thank you. I think it's wonderful and I'm going to keep it forever."

He gave her a look that made her feel thirteen, but she didn't care. She was falling for him, just a little bit, and a little crush never hurt anyone.

Cade returned with their dinner plates and he hadn't been exaggerating. The beef stir-fry was out of this world. She couldn't believe that this wasn't professionally prepared. It was seasoned to perfection, beef sautéed so that it was tender, while the vegetables still had crunch. "I have to hand it to you, this is delicious. I'm impressed."

"Good. You should let me take charge of dinners a couple nights a week. Give me something to do besides kill time until I can get things sorted with the Wyatts."

"Just what are you trying to sort out?"

His brow furrowed. His jaw hardened.

"You don't have to tell me," she said. "I'm sorry for pushing."

"It's just hard to talk about. I never know what to say."

"Whatever you feel like saying."

Cade seemed to be struggling to find the right words. "As you know DNA test results have said that Billy is my cousin."

"Which means Joe, Sam, and Tommy are your first cousins."

"Theoretically."

"Not theoretically. That's the way science works."

"But Sam and Joe don't trust the results—"

"That's ridiculous!"

"They want to take a DNA test themselves. They want the three of us to do it at the same time so they can see the results before I'm introduced to the rest of the family."

"So, what's the holdup?"

"We're going to do it next week, once Sam and Ivy are back from Idaho."

"It's only Thursday today. Why doesn't Joe just take the test?"

"I don't know, but it's what they wanted."

"You've come all this way—"

"Yes, but I don't want to just barge in and make demands. It will only create friction, and that's not how I want to meet my dad's family. Besides, I've waited twelve years for this. What's another few days?"

"Except that you have a right to know. I think it's selfish of them."

He smiled at her. "You're more of a hothead than I knew."

"I do have red hair."

"Well, I like your red hair."

She blushed and felt a tingly shiver rush through her. "Is that why you wouldn't let the doctor shave it at the hospital?"

"As well as the fact that it wasn't necessary." He rose, collected her plate. "I've got to call Willis, but would you want some dessert later? I picked up an apple crumble pie from Main Street Diner. Flo told me that was your favorite."

He'd brought home a pie that was her favorite. He'd made a dinner tray. He'd prepared dinner. A lump filled her throat. She didn't know how to take it all in. "You better stop spoiling me, Cade," she said huskily. "You'll soon make me unbearable."

"Sounds rather interesting," he said, taking the empty dishes into the kitchen.

CADE COULDN'T KEEP himself busy enough. Days passed far too slowly in Marietta. He wasn't a city guy. He'd been raised in Sheridan, Wyoming, but the majority of the last sixteen years had been spent in the Big Horn Mountains. The only years he'd been away from the Sundowner were during the years he served, and then whenever Dot had business. Cade always drove her to her meetings, except for the one time they flew to Chicago. She'd had a private plane take them from Sheridan and they stayed in her favorite hotel, a four-star property overlooking a massive lake.

Cade was anxious to return to the Sundowner. He missed his cabin, his horse, his work, his mountains. But the missing wasn't the only thing making him feel out of sorts. It was MerriBee. The fact that he wanted to be with her meant he couldn't let himself be with her, because he didn't trust himself not to ruin things. He wasn't sure what was happening between them, but there was definitely… something. An awareness, attraction, a slow, simmering tension that made his blood heat and his body ache.

He hadn't been drawn to any woman in a long time. Probably not since he and Polly ended their relationship, and that was three years ago.

CADE WAS OUTSIDE chopping wood.

Whack, whack, whack. The wood would crack, divide, and he'd start again.

MerriBee couldn't focus on anything but the sound of Cade working. She'd peeked out the window to watch him in the backyard. He'd stripped off his coat, and worked in an old gray sweatshirt, a black knit cap on his head.

He was strong and handsome. So appealing she didn't want to look away, but after she'd stared a long time, and soaked him in, she forced herself to move from the window and do something else. She hadn't yet figured out what to do.

Just knowing he was out there, working, splitting firewood for her fireplace, making things better for her, made her chest tighten and ache.

John had never been able to do any of those things. John had never been able to provide for her, or take care of her—not that she'd needed it. But still, it felt good to have someone here in the house, someone to talk to, someone to eat with. She'd miss the company when Cade left. She wasn't sure when that would happen, but sometime around Christmas, she knew that much.

MerriBee hopped down to the kitchen. She wasn't sure what she was going to do there, only that it was at the opposite end of the house from where Cade was working.

She reached into the freezer for one of the Christmas cookies she'd baked just before Cade arrived. It was one of the spritz cookies with a cinnamon in the middle. She nibbled on the cookie, feeling sensitive. There were so many feelings.

She was wishing. Hoping.

She was wanting things, wanting *something*, something the way she hadn't wanted since John.

But this wishing was also more than simply romantic feelings. This wishing reminded her of being a girl, when she'd get in trouble in school for not paying attention, which was wrong because she'd always paid attention. She could focus on the teacher and the lessons and still think about other things. She was smart, learned quickly, and so once she learned the lesson, she'd let her thoughts drift until there was something else to learn. It was hard to sit still otherwise.

She loved going to church, too, and looked forward to the annual bible camp, and summer camps, run by the church. She internalized all the lessons, particularly those about taking care of others, and loving your neighbor.

MerriBee was in seventh grade when her junior high

church group went skiing for a Saturday activity. With five big resorts just two hours from Spokane, winter sports were popular and she'd begun to enjoy skiing, not yet comfortable on advanced slopes, but fairly confident on the intermediate. She was flying down the mountain, feeling like a true skier, picking up speed, when she overshot a turn and went sailing off the groomed run into trees. She was never totally clear on what happened next—did she hit the tree itself? Or slide into the base?—but she fell in a tree well, the snow soft, deep and it covered her. Completely.

Buried by snow, unable to see or breathe, she panicked, digging this way and that, trying to find air, trying to find a way out. But the more she struggled, the more trapped she became until there was nothing else to be done. She was in His hands now. She stopped fighting. Stopped breathing.

The next time she opened her eyes, she was in a hospital. She'd been saved.

MerriBee wasn't sure why her life had been saved, but that week in the hospital left an indelible imprint. The doctors came and went, having very little time for anything or anyone, but the nurses did all the heavy lifting, physically, emotionally, spiritually. She appreciated—respected—the time they took out of their day to talk to her sharing stories, laughing, making sure she wasn't too lonely. By the time she went home, she knew that she wanted to go into nursing, too.

And she'd done just that.

She'd taken care of others, and loved, even when she knew the outcome was grim. John, for example. She still didn't regret marrying him. The year they were together was the best year of her life. But she'd gone numb after he died, and she'd been frozen ever since.

The deep freeze was thawing, though, and she was no longer numb. With her emotions returning, she didn't know what she was supposed to do... didn't know what she was supposed to feel.

Suddenly being single was confusing.

Suddenly this big house of hers overwhelmed her.

Suddenly she didn't like that she couldn't rest, couldn't slow down.

It was Cade who'd knocked the ice off her heart. Tough Cade who loved his life on a remote ranch in a different state.

Cade didn't share any of her beliefs. Cade didn't want what she wanted. Why was she falling for him? How could he be the one for her? They had nothing in common. They would never be able to have a life together. She shouldn't be drawn to him. Her heart shouldn't want him.

But it did.

Somehow they'd gotten through the weekend, and survived Monday. It was finally Monday night, and dinner was done, the dishes washed. MerriBee had helped with the dishes tonight. He'd washed, and she'd done her best to dry, but it took twice as long with her in the kitchen, in his way, all lips and eyes and beautiful hair. He couldn't focus when she was there, underfoot, making chitchat, laughing at his lame jokes, making him want her in the worst sort of way.

He wanted her up against the wall, his body pressed against hers, his mouth taking hers, kissing her until she melted. He wanted to taste her and feel her softness and let her warmth seep into him, easing some of his anger and frustration.

The DNA test had been scheduled for tomorrow at 11:30 a.m. in Bozeman, after MerriBee's nine o'clock appointment to get her stitches out. He'd looked up the address for the Bozeman lab, and the driving time, so he knew he could manage both without being late. But Sam had just texted, letting Cade know that he and Ivy were still in Idaho. They were buying the horse they'd gone to look at, but there was an issue with the bank and they'd need another day to get the financials settled.

Cade wasn't satisfied with a text, and called Sam, and they had a cordial conversation—the bank would only allow Sam to withdraw so much money in a day, but everything should be fine tomorrow—but after hanging up, Cade seethed.

He was fed up.

He faced the stove, hands pressed to the edge, and leaned into it, hard, letting it take his weight and more.

He wanted to hit something, beat something, fight.

He was sick of being stuck in this holding pattern. Sick of being dependent on strangers. He wanted answers, and he wanted them now. Not in a few days. Not in another week. Not when it was convenient for others.

He didn't know what caught his attention but suddenly he knew he wasn't alone and he didn't even have to open his eyes to know that MerriBee was in the kitchen with him but he didn't want to talk, and he didn't want to be nice. In fact, the only thing he wanted from her wasn't nice. He wouldn't be a gentleman. It'd be hot and dirty and way too rough for her. She was sweet. He was not.

"Cade?" she said, uncertainly.

"Yes, Bee?"

She made a soft sound, a muffled laugh. "Is that my name now?"

He straightened and turned around. She stood just inside the kitchen in her purple check flannel pajamas, her long hair caught up in a knot, a few tendrils damp, her cheeks were flushed, her skin dewy. She looked gorgeous. Kissable. Edible. "MerriBee is a mouthful," he said, biting back his anger, fighting his hunger. "Three syllables? Who has time for that?"

Her lips curved with amusement. "If you say it fast, you can make it two syllables. MerriBee."

"Bee's better."

"The *B* stands for Bradley, John's last name."

"And?"

"And nothing. Was just telling you."

"Okay."

She closed the distance between them, standing next to him near the stove. "What's upset you? You were in a good mood when I went to take a bath."

MerriBee didn't just look delicious, she smelled sweet and fresh, almond, vanilla, cinnamon, as if she were a warm Christmas cookie. "Sam's canceled tomorrow's appointment. He and Ivy are still in Idaho."

She put a hand on his arm. "I'm sorry."

He stiffened at the touch, her hand was light, but he wasn't in the best of moods, wasn't calm. With everything so roiled up inside of him, just that light touch made him feel hot, hard. She was standing far too close. He could see that violet fleck in her blue eyes. The impossible length of her black lashes. The faint crease in the middle of her soft lower lip. A lip that he wanted between his teeth. "Bee?"

"Yes?"

"If you don't want me to devour you, you might want to go."

Her head lifted, eyes wide. "Is that a joke?"

"No," he answered, his gaze riveted to her mouth, watching as the tip of her tongue peeked out, touched her upper lip. The things he'd like to do to her. The pleasure he'd give her. One night wouldn't be enough, either. He'd keep her in bed the next day, too. "I am very serious. You're in danger. I want you. I want to do a lot of very improper things to you, and if you're not ready to be thoroughly ravished, you should go. Now."

He heard her quick breath, and then her hand lifted, and after a slight hesitation she walked away.

MERRIBEE HAD MOVED back into her bedroom yesterday since she could handle putting more weight on her ankle. Her ankle wasn't healed, but she could carefully go up and down the stairs. But tonight she wished she was still downstairs, on a different floor from Cade, because she could hear him in his room, moving around, and she couldn't relax with him so close.

She also couldn't stop replaying his words in her head, and the intensity in his eyes. She'd felt his tension when she'd touched his arm, his body filled with leashed aggression. She didn't think the aggression was targeted at her. He was just angry. He needed an outlet. Any passion in his voice was a reflection of his frustration, not his interest in her.

He wasn't really interested in *her*.

And yet as she heard his voice again in her head, she shivered, aroused, curious, nervous, all of it. Of course, nothing would happen, but it was secretly exciting to fantasize. Cade was gorgeous and physical, mysterious and primal, and *he* wanted *her*.

He wanted to devour her, ravish her, do all sorts of very

improper things.

If anyone else had said it, she'd be turned off, but Cade wasn't just anyone. Cade was well, Cade, and she had begun to think about him all the time. And not in a platonic way, but in a—*I wish he'd kiss me so I'd know*—kind of way.

But what would the kiss tell her?

And what would she know?

MerriBee slept terribly, tossing and turning, dreaming dreams that she didn't normally dream. She kept checking the clock all night, and when it was four forty-five, she gave up trying to sleep, but as she lay there, she had a plan.

If the Wyatts wouldn't come to Cade, why couldn't Cade go to them?

Obviously, Cade couldn't just show up without a reason. But since she wasn't driving yet—although she could, she was fine now, but the Wyatts didn't need to know that—Cade would need to drive her to the Wyatts to drop off a thank-you gift for Joe and Sophie's cash donation and Sam and Ivy's coffee. She'd make some cookies and they could take them up, giving Cade a reason for being on the ranch, and hopefully a chance to meet Melvin Wyatt.

MerriBee liked her plan and pulled her favorite cardigan over her pajamas and carefully went down the stairs. The kitchen was warm, the heater on and the coffee was already made, but there was no sign of Cade.

She got to work right away. She turned the oven on, opened the fridge, took out butter and eggs, brought flour and sugar from her pantry, and began measuring the dry ingredients, while the mixer whipped the butter and sugar.

MerriBee had her first trays of spritz cookies in the oven when Cade appeared. "What are you doing?" he asked.

"Making cookies."

"It's not even five thirty. You don't even wake up until six thirty."

He still wasn't completely himself. His tone was clipped, his smile missing, but she wasn't taking it personally. The Wyatts seemed to be playing with his emotions, or at least, insensitive to what he was feeling.

"Instead of waiting for the Wyatts to come to you, why don't we go to them?" she asked as she topped off her coffee.

Cade didn't say anything, but he was listening.

"I have cookies for Sophie, a thank-you for her donation to my Christmas baskets. I'd love to be able to deliver them this morning, after I get my staples out." She sipped her coffee and looked at him over the rim of her cup. "Unless you have other plans?"

"That would tick off Joe and Sam for sure."

"So? Don't you want to see where your dad was raised? Don't you want to meet Mr. Wyatt?"

"That would really tick them off."

"But he's your grandfather. You have a right to meet him." She hesitated. "I know I'm overstepping. With you, it seems as if I always do, but you'd like him, Cade."

"Yes, but would he like me?"

"Without a doubt."

He said nothing and she didn't want to push him into doing anything he didn't want to do, because he was right, him just showing up could create a rift. "Maybe it was a bad idea—"

"No. I like it. I think we should do it. I want to meet Melvin. I've never had a grandfather before."

CADE COULD TELL that MerriBee was anxious about getting the staples removed, and she reached for his hand as the doctor approached, but it took no time at all to get them out, and then they were on their way.

"That wasn't so bad," she said, as they left Marietta Medical. "I thought it'd hurt. It didn't."

She wasn't limping very much, but they weren't walking fast. She'd dropped his hand after the procedure, but he almost wanted to take it back. Her hand felt good in his. She felt good next to him. She was a pretty feisty little thing. He hadn't expected that. All the Christmas stuff had him thinking she was sweeter than she was. But the woman had backbone, and a stubborn streak, too.

"So, what do you think?" she asked as they approached his truck. "Should we head out to Pray, or drive a different way? We don't have to drop in on the Wyatts. We could go to Clyde Park, Bozeman, Big Sky—"

"But you have freshly baked cookies to deliver," he said,

opening the door for her, giving her a hand up. "If we don't drop them off, I'll eat them, and the last thing my horse wants is me putting on some pounds."

She flashed him a grin. "Does your horse talk to you?"

"Not in words, but he has his ways of communicating."

"Then let's deliver those cookies."

It didn't take long before they were heading south on Highway 189, a road he was starting to get to know well. He also knew the right turn off for the Wyatt ranch, first following the exit to Pray, and then after the small town, he'd take a left on Diamond Road, and Diamond would take them up into the mountains. The roads were muddy in places and as they traveled higher, the mud turned to dirty snow and patches of ice.

Cade had driven on roads like this his entire life, the roads at Sundowner Ranch were the same—well, honestly, they were in better condition—but he wasn't being critical. Sundowner Ranch wasn't just a private ranch anymore, it served as a dude ranch during the late spring and summer months, and they had to keep the roads clear and in good condition for guests.

Cade slowed at a fork in the road, and MerriBee pointed to the right. He drove on through a thicket of aspens, the trees leafless, the bark stunningly white. As they cleared the aspens there were evergreens, and on the left was a new log cabin, two stories, the logs a golden honey.

"That's Joe and Sophie's," MerriBee said. "Joe built it for

Sophie after they married a few years ago. Melvin lives in the old log cabin up ahead."

"What about Sam and Ivy?" he asked, as two dogs came bounding out, barking.

"They have their own ranch here in the valley."

So, it would be Joe he'd have to deal with today, and hopefully Joe wouldn't be around. Through a clearing in the evergreens, Cade saw the roof of a much older cabin, as well as a barn in the distance. The dogs kept barking, dashing in front and then behind the truck as they approached the old cabin. "I think we've been announced," Cade said dryly.

"I guess we will find out who's here," MerriBee said brightly. "And the dogs just sound bad. Once you get out, they'll be fine."

Cade glanced at her, amused. "Is that how it works?"

"They're good dogs," she assured him.

Cade's gaze swept her lovely face with its earnest expression and felt his chest tighten. It felt as if she was going into battle with him, when he was the one who wanted to protect her. "They may be friendly," he said, "but stay put until I come around. Just in case they want your cookies."

The dogs sniffed him, and barked some more, a little less vigorously than before. Cade opened MerriBee's door and assisted her down. Her ankle was doing better, but there were patches of ice, and he didn't want to risk her slipping and sliding and reinjuring the ankle. Another dog, a young blond Lab, appeared from the side of the cabin, tail wagging, tongue hanging out of his mouth.

"What a cute pup," MerriBee said, greeting each of the dogs, but showering extra attention on the puppy. "Someday I'm going to have a dog, but it'd have to be a rescue dog that needs a home."

But of course that would be the kind of dog she'd get, he thought, checking his smile.

"Can I help you with something?" a tall white-haired older man said from the cabin's front porch.

"That's Melvin," MerriBee murmured.

Even if MerriBee hadn't said his name, Cade would have known. Melvin Wyatt looked an awful lot like an older version of himself.

MerriBee laced her fingers in his, giving him a little squeeze.

"Hello, Mr. Wyatt," MerriBee called. "It's MerriBee. I've brought some cookies, as a thank you—"

"What are you doing here?" Joe interrupted, marching toward them from the barn.

"Morning, Joe. How are you?" MerriBee asked with that radiant smile of hers.

"I thought we agreed not now," Joe said, closing the distance quickly, dogs moving to his side. His voice dropped. "After the test." He'd pitched his voice so that they were the only two that could hear him. "After we know."

Cade glanced at the older man on the porch. "I know." His eyes stung, hot and gritty. "Maybe you need all these hoops, but I don't. Maybe you can't see the family resemblance, but I can." He nodded toward Melvin who was coming down the steps. "Maybe you aren't my family, but he is. I don't need a DNA test to tell me that."

Cade dropped MerriBee's hand and crossed the gravel walkway, meeting Melvin Wyatt halfway. "Mr. Wyatt," he said, extending his hand. "My name's Cade Hunt and I have a few questions about my dad. I never knew him, but a recent DNA test leads me to believe he might have been your son."

Melvin took Cade's hand, and held it as he looked hard at Cade, his pale blue eyes searching Cade's face. And then he dropped Cade's hand and wrapped an arm around his shoulders. "You look just like my Samuel."

"Joe and Sam said that."

Melvin drew back to study Cade's face again. "I had no idea you even existed. If I had, I would have come find you years ago."

"Same," Cade agreed, ignoring Joe's ferocious face. "I don't know anything about my dad, but I'm hoping you can fill me in."

"Absolutely, son, come on in."

MERRIBEE SAT IN the kitchen with Summer, the Wyatt brothers' mom, and had a couple of the cookies she'd brought along with a cup of tea. Summer's arthritis was crippling, and she relied on a wheelchair more and more, making it difficult and since she couldn't get to town often, MerriBee filled her in on this year's Stroll. "I pretty much sold out of everything," MerriBee said. "It was probably the biggest crowd I've seen."

Summer commented on MerriBee's cast, and MerriBee told her how she fell, and how Cade came to her rescue and had been helping her out ever since. "He's a really good person." MerriBee paused, adding, "If he wasn't, I wouldn't have encouraged him to come here today."

"I'm sure he's a good person. He's the spitting image of his dad." Summer's eyes were pink. She was holding back tears. "I can't even imagine what Dad is feeling right now. I'm overwhelmed."

"Did you know Samuel well?"

"JC and Samuel were best friends. They were always together. I used to get mad at JC, complaining about Samuel always being around, I wanted some time alone with him—" She broke off, and smiled a watery smile. "Obviously, that wasn't entirely true. We ended up with four boys, so there must have been some alone time."

"Joe's not happy we're here," MerriBee said. "He and Sam wanted to get the DNA test first."

"There hasn't been one?"

"No, there has. Cade took one several years ago but he only recently got information that indicated Billy was his first cousin, and so Cade's in Marietta, trying to sort the family history out."

"But Joe and Sam have made it difficult for Cade."

"I think they're trying to protect Melvin from disappointment, in the event the DNA test Cade took was false."

Twenty minutes later, Cade and Melvin appeared in the kitchen. "We should go," he said simply.

MerriBee didn't know if something had happened, but now was not the time to ask. She nodded, and rising, said her goodbyes to Summer and then Melvin. Cade leaned over and kissed Summer's cheek and then he was holding the kitchen door open for MerriBee, and they walked out to his truck.

They didn't see Joe on the way out, and Cade was silent during the drive down the mountain. MerriBee chewed on the inside of her lip, wondering if everything was alright, but unable to read Cade's mood.

Once on the highway, Cade turned on the radio to a talk radio program, but the next moment turned it off again. MerriBee glanced at Cade once more, but again kept quiet. She was good at filling silences, but now wasn't the time. Cade clearly had a lot on his mind.

They were nearing the turnoff for Copper Mountain when MerriBee asked if he'd mind if they'd drive up to Miracle Lake.

He glanced at her, and then down at her foot. "You really think you're up for skating?"

"We could just watch. Maybe get a hot chocolate. I don't

think either of us are in a hurry to get back to the house."

"True."

The parking lot was surprisingly full but Cade was able to find a spot up the hill near a turnout for a popular hiking trail. He wouldn't let her walk down the hill, though, insisting on giving her a piggy-back ride. Down by the frozen lake, he lowered her onto an empty log and went in search of warm drinks. MerriBee watched him go, worried about him. What had happened during his conversation with Melvin?

What was said?

He was very much a tough, practical, hardworking man, but he had a soft side, a thoughtful side, and she knew the meeting today was a big deal. Maybe that was why he couldn't talk about it. Maybe he was trying to process his feelings.

She could see him at the hot chocolate hut, ordering their drinks, and her heart turned over, chest tender.

He was so handsome. She loved looking at him, watching him, watching him work, walk, move. He was all man, a very sexy man, and normally men like him weren't interested in her, but last night he'd said he was.

Did he still feel that way?

Just thinking about the things he'd said in the kitchen last night brought all the butterflies back. She was so aware of him now. The awareness made her restless. She wanted him to kiss her and wondered what he'd do if she kissed him. Maybe now wasn't the right time for a kiss, but perhaps tonight, or tomorrow...

MerriBee forced her attention to the lake. There were some very young skaters out, as well as a girl who looked like she competed. She was doing twirls and jump kicks and things MerriBee didn't know the names of. The girl couldn't have been much more than fourteen and yet she skated with such confidence. MerriBee was envious. She wished she could be young again and make different choices.

She'd choose differently.

She'd choose a family.

No one really wanted to grow up and grow old alone.

Cade appeared with their hot chocolates. Well, he'd bought one for her, topped with a mountain of whipped cream, and a plain black coffee for him. "You have no spirit," she said with mock severity, as he sat down next to her and handed her drink to her.

His shoulder brushed hers as he settled in. As he extended his legs, his thigh was pressed to hers. She suppressed a shiver. She wasn't cold, just excited.

"I'm not a hot chocolate fan," he said, glancing at her. "I've never had much of a sweet tooth."

"But you brought me home pie from the diner."

"Because you like pie."

"But you had some with me."

"Because you like pie," he repeated, reaching out to wipe her nose. "Whipped cream."

"What about cake? What kind would you get for your

birthday?"

"Whatever was cheapest at the grocery store's bakery. Usually, it was a day-old cake, which inevitably meant carrot cake, or a lemon cake."

"And you didn't like, either."

"It was fine."

Her eyes searched his. "I bet it wasn't, not to a little boy."

"As long as no one was drunk or crying, it was a good enough birthday."

Good enough. She swallowed hard, hating his childhood. "That sounds terrible."

His blue gaze warmed. "I survived."

"And found Dot," she said.

"You're adorable," he said with a shake of his head. "Is everyone charmed by you?"

"No. I scare some people with my intensity."

"That's impossible."

"No, I've heard some of the younger nurses talk. They dread having to work with me."

"Their loss," he said, leaning close, his lips covering hers in the lightest, most fleeting of kisses.

Just the brush of his mouth against hers sent a shiver up and down her spine.

She sighed and leaned toward him. "Could you please do that again?" she whispered.

"When you ask so nicely—" He didn't finish the sentence as his mouth covered hers in a kiss that was not light or fleeting. His mouth claimed hers, his tongue flicking at the seam of her lips, teasing, tasting.

Time slowed. MerriBee's head felt light, her pulse heavy. She arched closer, wanting more. Cade deepened the kiss, parting her lips, exploring her mouth, stirring every nerve ending as he did so. She was trembling when he broke off the kiss, and MerriBee blinked up at him, shaken. *That kiss...* It was everything and more.

MerriBee drew an unsteady breath, and then another, trying to calm her thudding pulse. She'd never been kissed like that in her life. She'd never felt anything so sensual, or so satisfying. And it had just been a kiss, on a log, by a frozen lake, in front of a dozen ice-skaters.

"What are you thinking, Bee?" he asked, his voice sinfully deep, and sexy.

"That you, um, kiss really good." She tried to look at him but couldn't quite meet his eyes. She felt hot and flustered... and good. Full of delicious sensation good. She'd never felt anything like this, never felt so warm, so soft, so full of yearning. Since John's death, she'd felt cold, frozen, but Cade's kiss made her tingle from head to toe.

She wasn't dead. Wasn't an ice cube. Wasn't any of those things she'd feared. Someone she'd dated while she was in nursing school said the reason she wanted to save the world was because she couldn't like herself. She'd been hurt, but she'd known he was wrong. She knew she just had to meet the right person. And then she met John.

And now Cade.

She reached up and lightly touched her mouth with her fingertips. Her lips were swollen, sensitive. "My lips are tingling."

"I've wanted to do that for a long time," he said, leaning forward to kiss the corner of her mouth.

A frisson of pleasure shot through her, making her shiver. "Why?"

"You have a mouth made for kissing. And I like you."

She wrapped her hands around her cup, still discombobulated. "You do?"

"I think I've made that abundantly clear this past week."

"And yet you told me to run last night. Flee."

"I don't want to ever presume, and I don't want to ever offend. I respect you too much."

Her gaze met his. "But…?"

"I've been wanting to kiss you ever since I walked in and out of that train room the first time. But not just kiss you. Sometimes I can't sleep at night because you're very much on my mind."

She looked away, out toward the skaters and the young teenage couple skating past, hand in hand. The boy was stumbling a bit, the girl was offering encouragement.

"Why do I make you nervous, Bee?" he asked, his deep voice quiet.

She turned her head and looked at him, into his eyes

which held her captive. Normally his irises were a cool, glacier blue, but they were warm now, intent.

"You're the first person I've kissed in five years," she blurted, deciding honesty was the best way. "Well, other than this peck good night three years ago, and I didn't like it, and didn't want to repeat it."

"But you like my kisses."

Heat washed though her, making her face burn. "I do."

"What about making love?"

She shook her head. "Haven't done that, either."

Cade's gaze remained locked with hers. "So there's been no one in your life?"

"Not since John died. I just… couldn't."

"That's a long time to be single."

"I've been busy. I work a lot."

"You don't get lonely?"

Her cheeks burned. Her lower lip throbbed a bit. She didn't know where to look. "I didn't miss dating, didn't miss relationships, at least not until you arrived. Now… I'm questioning everything, including never having a family. I'm almost thirty. There's no reason I couldn't have kids."

"When is your birthday?"

"December thirty-first." She looked from her cocoa up at him. "Born just two minutes shy of midnight."

"A New Year's baby."

"Mom said it was her worst New Year's Eve ever."

He grinned. "And now this year you turn thirty?"

She nodded and took a quick sip from her cocoa while watching the skaters go around. One little girl kept falling but every time her brother tried to help her up, she told him to go away. "It's just crossed my mind that maybe I need to rethink some of my decisions, maybe those decisions weren't healthy. Maybe I made them because I was grieving."

"And you're not grieving anymore?"

"I like to remember him now as he was when I first met him, when he was healthy and strong. I don't like remembering the end. It was heartbreaking."

They sat in silence for a long minute, the only sound that of the skaters on the ice, and their voices talking, laughing.

Finally, Cade stretched his legs out, propping one boot over the other. "My mom's death made me afraid of dying, not living. It seems like your husband's death had the opposite effect."

She'd never thought of it that way, but Cade was wrong. She shot a glance at him. He was focused on the ice and she used the opportunity to study his profile. He was so handsome he took her breath away.

"I thought John was my soul mate," she said quietly. "I thought I'd had my chance, and there probably wasn't anyone else for me out there."

Cade looked at her, their gazes locked. "You really think God only had one person for you?"

She made a soft sound. "I don't know anymore. Everything's changing. I'm changing. But it's scary. I liked having a focus, a direction."

"A world to save," he said.

"Yes." She smiled crookedly, waiting for him to laugh. He didn't. She glanced at him, eyebrow arching. "So, there you have it. My entire romantic history. Disappointed?"

He closed the distance between them, kissed her slowly, with bone-melting heat. "No," he said, when he ended the kiss. "There's nothing about you that disappoints me."

She didn't know what to say to that. A lump filled her throat. She slipped her hand through the crook of his arm.

He took her hand and held it in his. For the next few minutes, they just watched the skaters go around and around on Miracle Lake, and for MerriBee, it felt a little bit like a miracle of her own. She didn't think she'd ever feel this way again, and yet she was falling for him so hard and fast her heart felt almost sore.

"You know, I'm three years older than my dad was, when he died," Cade said, breaking the silence. "Melvin brought out some photo albums, showed me pictures of my dad, from the time he was born until the last rodeo before he died. It's uncanny how much we look alike."

"The DNA is strong," MerriBee said.

"It was comfortable talking to Melvin. I felt as if I've known him my whole life."

"I wondered how your conversation went."

"It went well. I really like him." Cade's voice deepened. "After all those years of not knowing, it's reassuring to discover I come from good people."

❦

THEY WERE ON the outskirts of Marietta when Cade's phone rang. He noted the name. Sam Wyatt. Cade was tempted to ignore it, but then decided it was better to just get the call over with. He answered on speaker. "Hello, Sam."

"I got a call from Joe. He's pretty upset," Sam said.

"Sorry about that."

"You're not. Otherwise you wouldn't have gone up."

"MerriBee had cookies to deliver."

"All you had to do was wait another few days, now Joe doesn't want you back, and Granddad's going to get caught in the middle—"

"Then tell Joe to get out of the middle. This isn't about him." Cade hesitated. "Or you."

"We'd agreed to a plan."

"A plan that was convenient for you."

"Joe's not going to want you back on the property."

"That's fine. Your granddad has my number. He can reach out to me when he wants." And then Cade hung up, because he wasn't going to be lectured by anyone, not even a Wyatt that probably was his cousin.

He glanced at Merribee who was looking stricken. "Relax. It's okay. I'm not worried."

"This isn't what you wanted, though."

"But I got the information I needed. I'm fine. I can head

back home without wondering about my dad."

CADE COOKED STEAKS for dinner, along with baked potatoes and a big side salad that could have been a meal in and of itself. When it was time to eat, he had her sit on the couch. "We're having a date," he said.

"We are?"

"Yes, you're going to sit on the couch with me."

"You're not weirded out by what I told you, earlier?"

He lifted an eyebrow.

"About the whole thirty-year-old emotionally frigid widow part," she said, although she was certain he knew exactly what she was referencing.

"Technically, you're a twenty-nine-year-old emotionally frigid widow, but I don't think you're emotionally frigid at all. I just think you weren't ready to move forward, and maybe you might be now."

"You think?" she asked, heat sweeping through her.

He pulled her onto his lap, facing him, and she stopped breathing. "Yeah, I do."

She made a little choking sound. He was hard and warm and her body was feeling everything.

"How's that feel?" he asked.

She was so hot she felt as if her skin would peel off any minute. "As if you like playing with fire."

He cupped the back of her head, drew her mouth to his,

and whispered against her lips, "Baby, I am fire."

And then he kissed her, and kissed her, and for the next half hour kissed her until all she could think was how much she wanted him. How much she needed him. And how much she loved him. He wasn't right for her—nothing about their lives made sense—but he'd appeared in her life and chipped the ice off her heart and when he left after Christmas, nothing would be the same.

CHAPTER SEVEN

CADE DIDN'T NORMALLY sleep in, but after the make-out session last night, they'd needed a cool down, and watched a thriller, which had MerriBee hiding her face against his chest for half the movie, which had been just fine with him. He'd held her, and looped her long hair around his hand, savoring the cool, silky feel of it. Watching a movie with Bee, feeling her in his arms, tucked against his chest, he felt calmer than he had in a long time. He also felt at peace. He'd met Melvin, he'd seen photos of his dad, he knew where his dad had been raised, and the values he'd had, and it settled something inside Cade, giving him room to feel other emotions, like this desire for Bee.

It wasn't all sex though. He could see them together, having a life together. It was the first time he'd pictured a future with anyone, but with her, he could see marriage, and a baby, possibly several babies. She'd be a good mom. She was giving and nurturing, but also strong, smart, funny. She'd love her kids but she'd be no pushover, and he could see them at the ranch, see them at Christmas, which was even stranger since he didn't like Christmas.

But with her, he'd want Christmas, and he wouldn't mind all the decorations. The kids would love them. Kids loved Christmas. He'd make sure his kids—their kids—had good Christmases. No fighting, no drinking, no gut-wrenching scenes that tore everyone's heart from their chest.

He didn't know anything about being a good husband, or a father, but he could learn. He and Bee were already friends. More than friends. He wanted her. Wanted to keep her with him. It was rather caveman-like, but it was how he felt. She was his, and he'd take care of her. No one else took care of her. No one else made sure she was safe. But he would.

It was after midnight when Cade finally fell asleep, and he slept in the next morning. He was still in bed at six when he got a call from Willis, but he was awake and alert the moment he answered the phone.

"She's sick," Willis said without preamble. "Seemed a little achy yesterday and wanted to skip the big family dinner and just go to bed early."

Even without saying her name, Cade knew Willis was talking about Dot. "Why didn't you call me last night?" he demanded, flinging back the covers and climbing from bed.

"Dot said she'd fire me if I did."

Cade stepped into his jeans. "She wouldn't fire you."

"She said it was just a little cold, and you're on your vacation—"

"How is she this morning?"

"She's back asleep but was awake earlier. She didn't want to eat anything. Em said she's running a fever."

"How high?"

"A hundred and two."

Cade swore silently, thinking that if it went much higher it would be really serious. "Has a doctor been called?"

"No one's coming out here in this weather. It's been snowing for two days."

"So you're not going to take her to a doctor, either?" Cade pulled a long-sleeve thermal shirt on, and then dug through the closet for a red flannel shirt.

"You know how she is about doctors. She won't go."

"I'm on my way."

"Why don't you wait and see how she's feeling later this morning?"

"You just said she has a fever. I'm not going to sit around here if she's ill."

"She's going to be fine. You know how tough she is—"

"I also know she's ninety-two, and she might be tough, but I remember last year—"

"I do, too," Willis interrupted.

"I'll be on the road in the next half hour."

MERRIBEE WAS JUST pouring her first cup of coffee when she heard Cade's footsteps on the stairs. He entered the kitchen fully dressed, coat on, hat on, packed duffel in his hand. Her heart fell when she saw he was planning to leave, throwing her back to a couple weeks ago when he'd come to say he wasn't going to stay.

He was leaving again.

A lump filled her throat. "You're off," she said, huskily, unable to hide the disappointment flooding her.

"Dot's ill. Willis just called. I need to head back."

Her gaze went to his duffel. It was tightly packed. She had a feeling he wasn't planning on coming back. She prayed she was wrong. "Did you pack everything?"

He nodded. "Not sure how long I'll be needed there."

"Have you been in touch with her doctor?"

"Dot's difficult that way. It's a fight to get her to go see anyone."

"The doctor won't come to her?"

"There's no one close anymore. Her old doctor made house calls, but the new one is a younger doc and lives north of Sheridan and doesn't make house calls. We can sometimes convince him to visit, but not in bad weather, and it's been snowing for a couple days."

"I'll go." The words were out of her mouth before she even thought about what she was saying. "I have extensive medical experience."

"She's not dying," Cade said.

MerriBee almost punched him. "I know how to keep people alive, too."

"I don't know when I could bring you back. It could be a

few days, could be a bit longer. It'd depend on how she is."

MerriBee mentally counted the days until Christmas. She'd normally start delivering her baskets a week from today. "I have nothing pressing until next week when I deliver my baskets. If you could get someone to drive me back in six days, maybe a ranch hand, I'd be able to take care of Dot and still get my baskets out on time."

Cade thought about it for a moment, then nodded. "If you're serious about going, I'll make sure you're back on the twenty-second."

"Perfect. Let me go pack. I won't need more than fifteen minutes."

While she packed both clothes and her nurse's bag, adding extra supplies just in case, more gloves, saline flushes, and sanitary items, Cade warmed up the truck, and cleared his windshield of ice. He carried her bags down and MerriBee quickly cut some slices of the cinnamon streusel bread which she'd pulled from the freezer last night, wrapped up the rest and tucked it in a lunch box along with a thermos of coffee for Cade, and water for her.

A half hour into the four-and-a-half-hour drive, Cade called Willis, wanting an update on Dot. Willis had Cade on speaker so Dot could hear the conversation. Dot was glad because it looped her in. It sounded as if Dot's fever was still the same, she was achy and needed some painkillers. She didn't have an appetite, and just wanted to go back to sleep.

After Cade hung up he glanced at MerriBee. "What do

you think?"

"If her fever gets any higher she should go to a hospital."

"She won't go, not unless she delirious and can't fight us."

"Fevers in seniors are usually related to a viral or bacterial infection. A viral infection could be the flu, bacterial a UTI, which is common for seniors, or something gastrointestinal."

"I shouldn't have left her."

"If she's not vomiting, and she isn't having difficulty breathing, it could be the flu—"

"Which is serious for someone her age," he said. "That's what she had last year and it turned into pneumonia. It happened so fast we didn't even know she'd gotten that sick."

"I'll be there monitoring her symptoms, and just knowing she's susceptible to pneumonia helps. I can call in antibiotics in advance, just in case—"

"Nurses can prescribe medicine?"

"If you're a nurse practioner, which I am."

"I didn't know."

She flashed a smile. "There was no reason for you to know. But I promise you, Dot will be in good hands. We'll focus on keeping her resting and getting a lot of fluids into her. I think having a canister of oxygen wouldn't hurt, as oxygen supplementation is often an important part of home care."

"We could pick up the medicine and oxygen in Sheridan,

it's on the way."

"I'll call both in now. Just need to look up the numbers."

The first hour of the drive was fairly clear, but clouds soon blanketed the sun, and the first snowflakes began to fall as they reached Billings. The snow grew heavier as they headed southeast.

"Will you be going home—to your parents—for Christmas?" Cade asked her as they finished their drive-through lunch. "Do you spend any of your holidays with them?"

MerriBee took his foil wrap and consolidated the trash. "Not anymore. If I visit, it's in the spring, usually for a late Easter or Mother's Day because the weather is better for driving, and I can go just for the day, or the weekend. There's not as much fuss, or expectations. Flowers, a card, maybe a gift. You eat, you talk, you leave." She shrugged. "Simple. Everyone's happy."

"You don't miss them, though? Your parents? Your brother and sisters?"

"I haven't lived near them since I graduated from college, and even when I was growing up, I was always a little outstep. I just was different. We never had a big falling out, but my parents found it difficult to relate to me. When I was a little girl, they wanted me to take ballet or baton twirling, and I'd wanted to try rock climbing. They hoped I'd be a Girl Scout, and I wanted to be a Boy Scout."

He grinned, amused. "Why?"

Her shoulders shifted. "I don't know, and I couldn't explain to them, or even myself. I just had this idea of who I was, which didn't quite align with their idea of who I should be. My sisters certainly didn't want to rock climb or be a Boy Scout. They didn't want to run track. I'm not sure why I did."

"But I'm sure they're proud of you now."

"They're relieved that I'm settled in Marietta. They just wish I was still doing neonatal care, instead of hospice."

"Why does hospice put them off?"

It was her turn to give him a sharp look. "For the same reason it puts you off."

"I'm not put off."

"No? Not even a little bit?"

He reached for her hand, fingers curling around hers. "I admit it threw me at first. It sounded depressing, but I've come to see what you do as a gift."

MerriBee exhaled hard, caught off guard. It was the nicest thing Cade had ever said to her, as well as the greatest compliment she could receive. "Thank you," she said softly. "That means a lot."

They drove in silence for several minutes, the windshield wipers swishing away the snow, the world outside the truck windows slowly being blanketed in white. "Can I ask you a question, Cade?"

"Of course."

"Are you happy?"

He squeezed her hand. "I'm not unhappy."

"That's not very convincing."

"I'm in a good place now. I wasn't always. I didn't live in a nice, suburban neighborhood. My parents both had addictions—Mom to pills, Dad—Jimmy—to drink and weed. I never minded if Jimmy smoked, though, as it mellowed him out. Liquor made him mean. Liquor, tequila in particular, meant fists would fly. Pot made him disappear into his head. Which was just fine with me."

"You didn't inherit any of their addictive tendencies?" She realized how the question sounded, and hastened to apologize. "Sorry. That wasn't phrased well. Being a nurse has taught me to ask questions: What are you on? What are you taking? What should I know about? When I worked in ER, lots of people came in, drug seeking, or hurting as they come down from whatever they were on."

"I have nothing to hide," he answered. "And no, I don't do drugs. I don't drink more than a beer or two every week. I don't like not being in control."

"Have you ever been married?"

"No."

"Have you ever been in love?"

"You're in a nosy mood."

"We have a long drive ahead of us."

He shot her an amused glance. "I can turn on the radio. But to answer your question, yes, I have been in love. I'm just not good at it."

She had to think about that one for a minute. "Love isn't a skill. I don't think it works that way."

"But I think it's a muscle. The heart's a muscle. If a muscle isn't used, it atrophies."

"Your heart has atrophied?" She couldn't hide her incredulity. She looked at him, her gaze skimming his big frame, his thick dark blond hair, his penetrating blue gaze. "No way. I don't believe that for a minute."

"I don't use it much. There's no need, not really."

"What about Dot?"

"Yes, but she's not a lot of work. It's easy to care for her."

He was so terribly handsome, impossibly rugged and male. She didn't think she'd ever found any man so appealing, and she glanced from his hand on the steering wheel to the flex of muscle in his thighs. His jeans wrapped his quads, outlining the hard, muscular lines. "Is love supposed to be work?" she asked.

He looked at her, eyebrow lifting. "Isn't it?"

"I don't think so." She smiled at him, smiling into his clear blue eyes and then her heart did a double thump, and her chest grew tight. *Because it's easy loving you.* She didn't say the words out loud, but they were in her heart, in her mouth, on her lips.

I love you.

This wasn't a crush anymore. It was so much bigger, and deeper than that, but MerriBee didn't know what to do with her feelings. He wasn't the person she thought she'd fall in love with. He wasn't the future she'd seen for herself.

Maybe love wasn't easy.

Maybe she'd gotten it all wrong.

AFTER AN HOUR stop in Sheridan, they reached the ranch midafternoon. The snow had stopped, and state transportation workers had been plowing the highway, but the road up to the Sundowner Ranch was still covered in snow. Cade's truck was able to make it with the snow tires, but just barely. He drove past a big circular drive, which led to a three-story log cabin lodge anchored with stone, to another road that was behind the lodge. A series of smaller log cabins, barns, and outbuildings dotted the road. Cade parked in front of the oldest cabin and was on a walkie-talkie he had in the truck, talking to one of the ranch hands even as he turned off the engine. "We need Warner Road cleared, and we need to keep it open," he added. "There are too many people here. It's asking for trouble to have the road inaccessible."

MerriBee heard a "yes, boss," at the other end and then Cade clicked off and looked at her. "You'll be staying up at the big house with Dot, but I thought you'd want to know where I'll be, so I'll show you my place and then we'll head up to the house together."

CADE KEPT THE tour brief as he was anxious to get to the

main house and see Dot. He picked up Bee's luggage, and
the purchases from the pharmacy and medical supply store in
Sheridan, placing them in the back of his black all-terrain
vehicle equipped for the snow. The ATV looked a bit like a
badass golf cart with its roof, second row of seats, and
windshield. The younger guys liked to ride around on the
snowmobiles, but Cade preferred his ATV.

The ATV started right up and MerriBee sat tall next to
him, her medical kit on her lap. She didn't look nervous, just
focused, gaze straight ahead, mittens clutching her nursing
bag, her long red ponytail hanging down her back.

They were greeted by Emma at the kitchen door, the one
he preferred using since he wasn't family and didn't want to
have to socialize with the Jameses. Emma and Willis were a
married couple who joined the ranch staff shortly after Cade.
Emma was twenty years older than Cade but he considered
her a good friend. "How is Dot?" he asked, giving her a hug.

"She says she's fine, but she's grouchy. Nothing you can't
handle," Emma answered. She turned to MerriBee. "I'm
Emma Love, cook, housekeeper, and friend to all."

MerriBee extended her hand. "Merri Bradley, or Mrs. B,
or MerriBee. Cade's taken to calling me Bee, so I pretty
much answer to everything."

As Emma shook her hand, she glanced from MerriBee to
Cade. "Does Dot know you've brought a friend?"

"Dot doesn't know I'm coming home, does she?"

Emma shook her head. "She'll give you grief for coming

home early, but I think she'll secretly be pleased. It's not been an easy two weeks—" She broke off at the sound of a barking dog. Actually, there were two barking dogs and it sounded as if they were barking at each other. "Dot will never admit it, but she's found it particularly stressful this year. She just doesn't handle the disruptions the way she used to."

"I knew I shouldn't have gone," Cade muttered.

Emma patted his arm. "But you're here now, and I think you're going to have to convince her that we should take her in to see the doctor, just to make sure everything's fine. Willis and I suggested it earlier but she wouldn't hear of it. But she's frailer than last time and we can't—"

"I know," he said firmly. "And I agree. That's why MerriBee's here. She's a nurse, and she's come prepared to take care of Dot."

"And if I have any concerns, about anything, I will insist we take Ms. Warner to a hospital immediately. We won't be messing around. Has she been taking a lot of fluids? Is she making many trips to the bathroom?"

"She doesn't want to drink, but I've been forcing her to drink eight ounces every ninety minutes," Emma said. "I've kept notes since yesterday on how much she's taking in because last year I didn't, and none of us realized how dehydrated she was."

"I'd love to see your notes once I've had a chance to introduce myself to her," MerriBee said. "And I'll be staying with her at night, so you can get your rest."

"We might want to take turns," Emma answered.

"Count on me," Cade said. "I'm back now, and I'm not going anywhere."

CHAPTER EIGHT

AT THE TIME, MerriBee didn't think anything of Cade's words—*I'm back now, and not going anywhere*—but he said a variation of them several times over the next few days and she realized he meant it.

He wasn't going to leave Dot, or the ranch, again. He'd send her back to Marietta with one of the ranch hands, maybe even Willis. He hadn't wanted to leave the first time, and now being back, and having met Melvin Wyatt already, Cade had no reason to leave again.

MerriBee thought about this a lot as she sat in Dot's room. The first day MerriBee was there, Dot slept a lot, but by late on the second day, she was more awake, as well as hungry. Emma made her a Mexican meatball soup for dinner, which she seemed to enjoy, and then asked Emma for chicken taco soup for lunch the next day, and by dinner the third day, Dot's fever was gone and she didn't want any more soup, but rather "real food."

"You can also stop hovering so much," Dot said, summoning Cade, MerriBee, and Emma. "I'm fine, and tomorrow I'm going to get out of bed—"

"For part of the day," Cade said.

She shot him a frosty look. "I don't believe I made you the boss of me, Cade Hunt. Just because you're back, doesn't mean you're calling the shots."

"No, but if you get out of bed for too long, Alistair and his family will troop in here with their little dogs and—"

"That's fine. I'll keep to my room. I won't go too far. I'm feeling better but not ready for Mitz and Bitz at my dinner table yet."

MerriBee fought a smile because she'd met the little dogs and their names were Mitsy and Bitsy—sister dogs for sister girls—and they were as spoiled as they sounded. "If you're bored," she said. "I can read to you, we can play a game of Scrabble—"

"How about gin rummy?" Dot suggested.

"Gin rummy it is," MerriBee said.

"I'll find the cards," Cade said.

"I'll send up some spiced cider and cookies," Emma said.

Dot waved her wrinkled hand, stopping her. "Do you have any more of the cinnamon bread with the streusel filling? I had a slice yesterday and liked it very much."

"That was MerriBee's bread," Emma said. "It's all gone, but we have pumpkin bread—"

"No, I'd like the cinnamon bread. MerriBee can give you the recipe."

"Actually, it's not written down, I just remember it. But I can go make a batch right now, and Emma could make notes, and then she'll have the recipe for the future," Merri-Bee said.

"Which means you're stuck playing gin with me," Cade said, returning with a deck of cards. "But, Dot, be forewarned. I will show you no mercy."

Dot's lips pursed, a teasing glint in her eyes. "You never do. I still beat you anyway. You're no match for me, but I respect you for trying."

NOW THAT SHE was feeling better, Cade was glad to have some time with Dot.

He set up the small folding card table from her closet and positioned the chairs so that her back was to the window. He broke the deck, shuffled the cards, and then quickly dealt their hands, flipping the top card on the remaining pile. "How are you feeling, really?" he asked, sorting his cards.

"Fine. Why wouldn't I be?"

"No need to be so sassy, Miss Warner."

She took the up card, looked at him pointedly over her hand. "No need to treat me like an invalid. I'm going to die someday, but it's not today, and it's not this year. I'm planning on sticking around for a long time." She discarded a card from her hand.

He took her discarded card, then set down one of his own. "That's reassuring. It's good to know I'll have a job a few years more."

She didn't want his card and took one off the pile. "You don't think Alistair would keep you on?"

Cade snorted. "No. Do you?"

"No." She discarded. "Which is a shame since you know this place better than anyone here."

"I think Willis knows it pretty well, but I do think I care for it more." He took her card, put down one from his hand. "It's been home for so long now."

"No matter what happens, you'll land on your feet. You're smart, hardworking, you understand what it takes to make a ranch successful. Every Western property would want you, and I'm sure would scoop you up." She drew one from the pile. "Just the way you're scooping my cards up."

He laughed as he reached for her newly discarded card. "I like your cards."

"Well, stop." She frowned at her cards, studied his discarded card, and took it. "Don't know why I did that. I need to focus and stop all the chitchat."

Cade didn't take her discard this time, and instead reached for the pile. "We will just play in silence. Don't want you to accuse me of taking advantage of a senior citizen."

"Ha! Now you sound like Alistair." She took a card off the pile, frowned, set it down. "He had the cheek to suggest that it was time he began to be part of the decision-making around here. Not sure why he thinks he should have a say."

Cade took her card. "Thank you for that." He laid his

hand down so she could see. "Gin."

Dot frowned at his cards and then at hers before quickly counting up the points, telling him to write it down.

"I'll just keep a tally in my head," he said, passing the cards to her so she could shuffle the deck.

Her hands might have a quiver, but she was still strong, and she shuffled crisply so the cards snapped as they fell.

"What decision-making does Alistair want to be part of?" Cade asked, picking up his hand.

"About the ranch, the future, my future." She arranged the cards in her hand. "Told me he's done some research and there are some wonderful retirement homes where I'd be quite comfortable." She looked at Cade over the rim of her glasses. "In Silicon Valley. Can you imagine? Me, there? It's never going to happen."

Cade picked up the up card. "You belong here."

"Exactly. I was born here. I intend to die here." She took the card he set down. "By the way, I have a very good hand, so be careful. No crying when I show you how it's done."

He laughed, a low rumble. "I'll try not to unman myself."

"Good. I've had enough of that these past few weeks." She didn't want the card he'd just discarded and took one off the top of the pile. "It's not been a good visit. I shouldn't tell you this, but I'm ready for them to go."

"The little dogs?"

"They're a metaphor for everything that's wrong." She

took his next discard, put one down from her hand. "Not just with them, but society. We're creating a world full of ninnies. People without courage, conviction, or backbone. And if I see one more person, taking one more self-portrait, I'm going to lose my mind. How many photos does one need of oneself?"

"Excellent questions, Dot, questions I don't have an answer for." He took a card off the pile, and then set one down. "Gin. Sorry, Dot. I don't think you shuffled very well."

"I shuffled well. The fates are just favoring you today." She pushed her cards at him. "I can't concentrate. You count it up."

He did and added the points to the tally in his head. As he began shuffling, he asked her, "Why do they think California would be a good place for you?"

"They say they can take care of me that way." Her voice sharpened, indignant. "And yet they're the ones that need taking care of. I never told you this, but Alistair needed money earlier this year. It was the first time he asked, but it was a sizable amount. He said he needs to speak with me privately, before they leave, and I have a feeling he's going to ask for more. I could be wrong. Maybe he and Abigail are divorcing. Maybe Paris wants to become a cowgirl. But my gut says, it's a financial request, and my gut also says, I will never, ever agree to be under their protection."

Cade slowly shuffled, once, and then again. "I want to

send them packing."

"Just another week or so."

"Do they have to come next year? They're not good for you. They create stress and bring germs and get you sick."

"I don't know," she said after a moment, and then gestured impatiently. "Deal. This hand is mine. Winner takes all."

They didn't talk much that hand, and Cade was just one card shy of gin when Dot put her cards down. "I won," she crowed. "I knew all your talking was distracting me. Next time I'll tape your mouth shut." And then she reached across the table, patted his hand, and winked. "You're a good man, Cade Hunt. Thank you for putting up with me."

He turned his hand over, gave hers a gentle squeeze. "Thank you for giving me a home."

THAT EVENING AFTER dinner, MerriBee slipped out of the big house to spend some time with Cade in his cabin. She was tired, but so glad Dot was on the mend. MerriBee couldn't imagine Cade's worry if things had turned serious. It was obvious that Dot was his world, she was more of a grandmother to him than boss, and she understood why he didn't want to leave the Sundowner Ranch. She wouldn't ever dream of asking him to leave, either. Certainly not for her. But at the same time, this wasn't MerriBee's home. The vast ranch was beautiful, and the mountains majestic, but there were no hospitals close. The biggest city was Sheridan and that was an hour drive from the ranch cabin.

But she didn't have to think about any of that yet. She had another few days here before she'd return to Marietta and she'd enjoy every minute she could with Cade.

Entering his cabin, she smelled popcorn, and closing the front door behind her, spied the fire crackling in the huge stone fireplace. "I'm here," she called, peeling off her coat, and removing her fur-lined boots.

"Make yourself comfortable," he said. "Just getting our refreshments."

She took a seat on the big leather couch before the fire, and wiggled her toes, admiring her candy cane socks. She had dozens of holiday socks but hadn't been wearing them in Marietta, and it was only when it was time to pack, that she remembered them.

Cade appeared with a big cutting board that he was using as a tray. On the board was a large stainless steel bowl filled with fresh popcorn, and two steaming mugs. The mugs were a practical brown. "No Christmas tree mugs?" she said, taking one.

"And no Christmas decorations, either." He placed the cutting board on the big leather ottoman and sat down next to her. "But it's buttered popcorn, and two cups of Baileys and decaf coffee. With whipped cream."

She grinned at him. "Which is almost as good as Christmas."

"I will not be baited," he said, reaching for the remote. "Tonight I shall take the high road because we are watching a Christmas movie."

"We are?" She scooted closer, excited.

"My favorite Christmas movie."

"I didn't know you had one."

"Of course I do. Everyone does."

The TV came on and she could see the screen. The movie had already been selected and was ready to go.

Die Hard.

She looked at Cade, not sure if she was disappointed or entertained. "You're not joking, are you?"

"No. It's a great Christmas movie," he said, completely serious. "So many good things happen in it. It has a great ending, a happy ending, and the good guys win. What more could you want?"

She leaned against Cade's chest and curled her legs up under her. That was an excellent question, she thought, as he pressed play. *A happy ending and the good guys win.*

He was right. What more could one want?

DOT PLANNED TO rejoin her family downstairs Saturday for lunch, and MerriBee was pretending to knit in the corner by the large bay window but was actually staying close in case Dot needed a hand while dressing. Dot's bedroom was enormous, with an equally large attached bathroom and closet, and so it was easy to sit in a corner and not be in the way.

Dot was wearing a long western-style skirt with a cashmere sweater, her turquoise jewelry and was in the process of putting on her boots when she sat down at the edge of the bed with a tired sigh. "I hate asking for help—"

"I'd love to." MerriBee was on her feet and crossing the room quickly. "I thought I'd be needed much sooner," she said, kneeling at Dot's feet and helping her get one sock on, and then her boot, and then the other, glad she could use her left fingers again but ready to lose the cast. "You're in excellent shape."

Dot looked pleased. "Good, because I intend to be around for quite a few years yet."

"And if you keep exercising and doing your strength training, you should be. You're only out of breath because you've been in bed for a few days, but by this time next week, you'll feel like yourself, ready to rule the world."

"Ha! I am ruling the world already." Dot took MerriBee's hand and allowed herself to be drawn to her feet. She needed a moment to balance herself, and then she was good. "Now, what are you and Cade up to this afternoon? Neither of you should be working."

"I think he is, though, and I'm happy to—"

"Nonsense. He's taking you on a sleigh ride."

"I don't think—"

"You don't have to. I've got it handled."

MerriBee laughed, and after a moment, Dot laughed, too. "There are benefits to getting old," Dot added when she'd caught her breath. "You get to call the shots, and you don't have to listen to anyone you don't want to."

"I hope I didn't offend."

"No. Not at all. I like you. You're just what the doctor ordered."

IT WAS A real sleigh, pulled by real horses, through real powdery white snow. With the days so short, the sun was already sinking lower in the sky, illuminating the scattered clouds and painting the horizon rose gold. Cade had a big blanket for their lap, and he'd brought thermoses of hot chocolate and he drove the sleigh with expertise, sending them gliding across what must be meadows in summer. They traveled over a low hill and down a gentle slope to circle a small frozen pond and then through scattered evergreens before reaching another clearing, where they stopped to sip hot drinks and let the horses rest for a bit.

"What was college like?" he asked, filling two cups with the hot cocoa. "What did I miss?"

He was drinking hot cocoa with her today but she didn't say anything about it even though she wanted to tease him because she suspected he was doing it for her. "A lot of classes, a lot of studying."

"I thought college was supposed to be a party. Everyone's

having a good ole time."

"Maybe for others, but I wasn't there to have fun. I was there to learn something important, so I could do something important. That's what I wanted, and what I did. And fun…?" She hesitated, then shook her head. "I don't seek out fun. But somehow fun finds me… just look at you."

"No one would describe me as fun," he said.

"I would and do." She snuggled into his side. "I have fun with you. But you're also a good person. You're strong, thoughtful, observant, practical. I appreciate those more than someone just looking for a good time.

"You forgot how handsome I was," he said, tweaking her nose.

"That's a given," she retorted. "But I don't want to flatter you too much. You might get a big head, and then you'd need a new hat—"

He kissed her, silencing her. "You're one goofy girl."

"I know." She looked up at him, searching his blue eyes, wondering what he thought about. He was often quiet, often a little distant and detached. "What matters most to you?"

"Dot," he said without hesitation. "The ranch. My work. Finding my sister, making sure she's okay." His lashes dropped, concealing his eyes. "And then there's you."

A lump filled MerriBee's throat and she swallowed hard. She hadn't expected that. She hadn't realized his feelings were quite so strong. "You haven't known me that long."

He shrugged. "Dot changed my life in one day. Why

can't you?"

She had no answer for that, and Cade gave the reins a shake, and the horses were moving again and they made their way back at a brisk pace, the sleigh covering ground quickly. They were definitely traveling a real road, as it was smooth with no obstacles. On the way back, Cade pointed out different places to her. "In summer we take guests on this road to a fire pit for a s'mores night and campfire stories. We also have a picnic area with lots of tables for our weekly barbecue." He pointed to a slope opposite them. "On the other side, is a spot for archery, and further down is a river, frozen now, but it's popular in summer for fishing."

"But you don't have to do all of that?"

"My job is mostly behind the scenes. Willis is the main contact for the dude ranch, from bookings to greeting folks and checking them in. I hire and train the summer help, make sure horses are healthy, manage the working part of the ranch, and keep an eye on logistics. I get introduced each Sunday night when the new guests arrive—"

"The dude ranch has a set schedule?" she interrupted.

"Sunday to Sunday, from Memorial Day to Labor Day. We have a couple weeks in September where we host special-ty camps, and then we're back to just being a private ranch until the following year."

"So, this was your college," MerriBee said, as the big log cabin house with the massive stone chimney came into view. "You learned what you needed here."

Cade slowed the pace. "The army helped, too. Taught me to accept responsibility for myself, not to blame others. It also taught me how to work with others, and be a team, something that has proven essential for running a ranch the size of Sundowner."

"Do you ever get bored here? Do you ever find it the same old routine?"

HE RUBBED HIS palm over her knee. "No. I enjoy being outside, and you've seen my toys—the ATV, the snowmobile, the truck, my horse—I like it all. Sometimes I feel guilty that it doesn't feel like work to me."

"That's the best kind of job," she said, slipping her fingers through his.

"Are you dreading going back to work?" he asked.

"No. I'll be ready for it. I like being busy."

"But first your Christmas baskets."

"Yes."

He said nothing else, and she didn't, either, her heart suddenly heavy, her eyes hot with tears she wouldn't let fall. For a few minutes there was just the sound of the horses' hooves kicking up snow and the jingle of the bell on the front of the sleigh.

"Dot likes you a lot," Cade said as they approached the main house.

"I like her, too. I love her stories. I could listen to her all day."

"That's how I know she likes you, she talks to you. She has virtually nothing to say to Alistair and his family. Their meals together are incredibly awkward. I don't know how any of them stand it."

"But it's a gorgeous place to come for Christmas. I can see why they return every year."

Cade's walkie-talkie, tucked beneath the sleigh bench, crackled to life. "Cade, are you there?"

Cade answered. "I am, Willis. What's up?"

"You have a guest here, waiting to see you."

Cade frowned. "I have a guest."

"He said his name is Tommy Wyatt, and he's your cousin."

❦

CADE SAW BEE'S stunned expression but deliberately kept his blank as he turned off the walkie-talkie and stowed it beneath the seat. "Did you know he was coming?" she asked, pulling the blanket up higher to her chest.

"No. Should be interesting. Haven't met this one yet."

"He's the youngest."

"So I've heard."

"Why is he here?" she asked.

"No idea." Cade slowed in front of the big house, and then drew the horses to a stop. He turned to look at her. Her blue-green eyes were enormous. "No reason to worry," he said. "I'm not worried."

"Yes, but you're dropping me off here. That means..." Her voice faltered. She made a face. "It means you don't want me there."

"It means Dot is probably looking forward to your return—"

"She doesn't like me that much."

"Yes, but she likes you better than the Jameses." He chucked her chin. "And I'd feel better if you were with her, while I go see Wyatt."

She sighed. "His name is Tommy. He's very nice—"

"Just like Sam and Joe?"

She ignored this. "And in case you've forgotten, you're a Wyatt, too."

"I don't know what I am, and honestly it doesn't matter. Don't fret. Make Dot think we had the most romantic sleigh ride—"

"We did, didn't we?" she interrupted, looking at him in a way that made him want to kiss her again. She was perfect, at least, perfect for him.

"Yes, we did," he said, smiling down at her. "The only thing we didn't do was sing carols as we dashed through the snow, but it's baby steps, you know."

"I do know."

He climbed out of the sleigh and reached in to lift her down. "But you're right about the other thing, if there's going to be trouble with *Tommy Wyatt*," he said, emphasizing the name for her benefit, "I'd rather you not be there."

"Don't do anything stupid." She patted his chest, worry in her eyes.

Cade smoothed a finger across her pink cheek. "Babe, everything's going to be fine. I'm not worried." He kissed her briefly, and then kissed her again, this one a slow, warm, lingering kiss that made him want to never let her go. "I'll find you when he's gone," he said.

"Promise?"

"Promise." Cade waited for her to disappear inside before grabbing the walkie-talkie and calling for one of the young hands to come take the horses and sleigh. If Cade was going to meet Tom Wyatt, he wasn't going to arrive looking like Santa Claus.

CHAPTER NINE

MERRIBEE DID NOT want to go into the big house, nor did she want to walk through the front door and be greeted by the sight of the Jameses gathered in the living room, sipping cocktails in front of the towering Christmas tree, anticipating dinner. The entire scene reminded her a little too much of the Crawley family in Downtown Abbey in their formal dress waiting for the butler to call them for dinner. Only in this case, Willis was the butler and seeing the family without Dorothy Warner didn't strike her as right. Willis wasn't their servant, and Emma wasn't their housekeeper or maid and this was Dot's personal home. Even on vacation they ought to help, at the very least, set the table, and clear the table, and not expect one woman to make a feast every night and then do all the cleanup on her own.

"Where is Miss Warner?" MerriBee asked one of the twins who was just a few years younger than her, thinking it was Paris, but it could have been London. Both of the young women were glamorous and impeccably dressed.

"I don't know." The blonde looked around, as if just noticing that her great-aunt wasn't there. "I don't know where she went. Maybe in the library, or maybe upstairs?"

MerriBee thanked her and was just about to continue on when a little Pekinese came running down the stairs, followed by the second Pekinese, barking wildly. The second one reached the bottom of the stairs and stopped barking long enough to squat on the antique wool carpet at the foot of the stairs and relieve herself.

"Oh Bitsy," London or Paris cried, picking the little dog up, and giving her a kiss, once, and then again. "Naughty, naughty!" And then she turned to MerriBee and said most apologetically, "Would you mind taking my cocktail napkin and dabbing that for me? Aunt Dorothy is so fussy about her old things. I don't want her to scold Bitsy again."

MerriBee opened her mouth to protest, and then closed it quickly, because if she hadn't, she would have laughed out loud. "No. I can't," she said. "That's your job. It's your dog." And then she went to the library thinking she'd start there in her search for Dot.

Dot was there, too, sitting at the huge mission-style oak desk, papers and file folders in front of her. She glanced up as MerriBee entered. "How was the sleigh ride?" she asked, squaring some of the loose sheets of paper.

"Wonderful." MerriBee began to unwind her scarf and then unfasten her coat. "I hope we weren't gone too long."

"You don't work for me, MerriBee, you're my guest, not my employee. I was counting on you ending your ride in a dinner for two by a cozy fire someplace."

MerriBee smiled and placed her coat and things on the back of a sturdy oak chair. "First of all, I don't think of you as my employer, but rather as Cade's favorite person, which means I value you highly. And secondly, Cade has a visitor and he wanted to dump me on you while he met with this person."

Dot looked intrigued. "Who is this person? Do you know?"

"Tommy Wyatt, the youngest of his four cousins."

"You know the Wyatt family?"

"I do."

Dot pointed at one of the big chairs facing her desk. "Sit and tell me all you know. Cade hasn't been very forthcoming."

"I think it was a challenging visit to Marietta. He wasn't able to accomplish as much as he wanted—"

"Then why didn't he stay longer?"

MerriBee wasn't about to make Dot the excuse. "I think he had enough of Joe and Sam's highhanded ways. He didn't like how they were keeping him from his granddad, Melvin Wyatt, but Cade finally did get to see him, and I think Cade will probably have a relationship with Melvin in the future. The rest of them... I rather doubt it."

"That bad?"

"Being raised as an only child, I think Cade isn't interested in birth order and pecking order, never mind being told what to do by men his own age."

"You have brothers and sisters?"

"One brother, two sisters," MerriBee answered.

"You're close to them?"

"No. Unfortunately." She wasn't sure if Dot wanted more, but she didn't necessarily want to say more about her family.

Dot was ready to move on, too. "And now Tommy's here."

"Yes."

"Perhaps he should join us for dinner. He's come a long way. I imagine he's hungry."

"I don't think Cade would like that."

"I'm the one inviting him to dinner, not Cade." She paused, steepled her fingers. "But I do think we should have you and Cade join us, too. My family is restless and tired of each other's company. My great-nieces are thoroughly bored. Having new guests at the dinner table should help." Dot looked at MerriBee expectantly. "Is Tommy single?"

"I believe so. Well, at least, he's not married. I don't know if he's in a relationship now. We're not that close."

"Is he attractive?"

MerriBee pictured him and nodded. Tommy was the best looking of the bunch, a younger version of Joe, fairer, more relaxed, more entertaining. "Tommy is quite fun. He has a good sense of humor."

"Perfect. That's exactly what we need. I'll call Cade and let him know. They'll need to freshen up." She reached for the phone on the desk and then hesitated. "And you should go freshen up, too. We're not excessively formal at dinner, but I do frown on snow gear."

MerriBee rose, dismissed, but also amused as she knew she was in Dot's good graces.

Then Dot held up a finger. "Also, let my great-nieces know that as we have guests tonight, they'll be leaving their pets upstairs in their kennels. It's one thing for the little dogs to sit at the table when we're alone, but I won't have my family embarrassing Cade in front of his family."

As MerriBee headed for the door, she pictured the Pekinese squatting on the antique rug and silently applauded Dot's decision.

CADE HADN'T EVEN been able to introduce himself before Tommy Wyatt came striding out of the shadows to introduce himself. "Had to meet you, and apologize for my brothers. Considering they both have wives, you'd think they'd be more civilized."

Cade had been prepared for a fight, not Tommy's friendly smile or surprise hug. He didn't quite know how to respond to the warm greeting.

"I've never had a cousin before," Tommy added, stepping back, hands slipping into his coat pockets. "At least my brothers got one thing right, you do look like Sam."

"What brought you this way?" Cade asked. "Didn't you

just wrap up the NFRs?"

"I did. But I was disappointed I didn't get to meet you, so thought I'd come find you, let you know we're not all bad. In fact, Joe and Sam aren't bad, but they're big brothers, which means they think they know everything and like to call the shots."

Cade gestured to his cabin. "Want to come in? Get warm?"

"Would love that. Thank you. It is cold."

Inside the cabin Cade built up the fire and offered Tommy a beer, but he said he'd rather have coffee, if Cade didn't mind. "You're not driving back tonight are you?" Cade asked.

"No. Hoped you might have a couch for me and then I'll head back in the morning. I don't want to be in your way."

"You're not in my way." The words were out before Cade thought them through, but it was true. He liked this Wyatt, liked his ready smile and quick laugh. Never mind that he'd just driven four and a half hours to introduce himself. "How were the roads?"

"Rough outside Billings. The wind was kicking it up."

Cade stepped into the cabin's snug kitchen and was just starting to make a fresh pot of coffee when the phone rang. It was his landline which was necessary up here in the mountains where cell coverage was spotty, if that. He could see the number calling, though, and knew it was Dot. "Everything okay up there?"

She immediately launched into a speech that turned into an invitation that he couldn't refuse. When she finally paused for breath, he politely told her he couldn't speak for Tom, only to be cut off. Cade listened again, his gaze meeting Tommy's across the room. Tommy shrugged, apparently unconcerned, and Cade covered the phone with his hand and asked Tommy how he felt about joining Dorothy Warner and her family for dinner. "Merri Bradley will be there, too," he added. "It will be a crowded table."

"Sounds fun."

Cade gave him a look as if to say *you're crazy*, but uncovered the phone and told Dot that they'd be there at six. "Promptly," he agreed, echoing her words. "I know you don't like to be kept waiting."

After hanging up, he looked at the coffeepot and then at Tommy. "We're supposed to be joining her at six. Which in her mind is ten to six. That only leaves us ten or fifteen minutes to shower and dress." Cade saw Tommy's expression and smiled ruefully. "Not in a tuxedo or anything, but a button-down long-sleeve shirt if you have it, clean Wranglers, shiny belt, boots."

"Have an extra shirt? I only brought long-sleeve thermals and outdoor flannels—" Tommy broke off. "Speaking of flannels, I have something for you. Granddad sent it with me." He disappeared through the front door, returning a few minutes later with his backpack and duffel. From the backpack he drew out a folded blue paid wool shirt. "This is an old shirt, was Granddad's from the 60s or 70s, but my uncle Samuel took it from Granddad's closet to wear somewhere and then never gave it back. It became Samuel's favorite shirt, and when he died, Granddad found it hanging in his closet. He took it home with him, and he's kept it all this time, but thought you might like to have something your dad used to wear."

Cade wasn't a crier, and he didn't choke up, but as he unfolded the shirt and looked at the old Pendleton tag in the collar, and felt the worn wool, emotion bottled inside his chest, and his throat thickened. He swallowed around the emotion, fighting to keep his feelings in check. "A true Wyatt shirt," he said, voice rough.

"Your dad's and granddad's," Tommy said.

Cade looked at Tommy. "Why didn't you need me to take a DNA test?"

"Because you already did. You've matched with Billy on that family site. You didn't make it match, technology did. He showed me his page when we were in Las Vegas. Well, his wife showed him the page, and then they both showed me."

"So, you believe me."

"Everyone believes you. Sam and Joe were just worried about Granddad, but they knew, they did, that you were family. All you have to do is look at you. It's written all over your face."

Cade held up the shirt, inspecting the vintage plaid. It

was a large, which was his size. It was also his favorite kind of shirt. "Thank your grandfather for me."

"Why don't you give him a call tomorrow? He's your grandfather, too."

🍎

TOMMY WYATT PRETTY much single-handedly saved dinner. Smiling, Cade watched him from across the table joking with the youngest Jameses, teasing and flirting with the twins, and talking stock market and the economy with Alistair James and his oldest son.

"How is it you know so much about Wall Street?" Alistair's son, Nathaniel, asked Tommy. "Where did you get your education?"

"Self-taught," Tommy said. "Just find it interesting."

"And you never went to college?"

"No, sir. Just the college of hard knocks." But Tommy's smile was wide and easy, and it crossed Cade's mind that that was also his gift. Not everyone was good with people, and not everyone had a head for numbers, but Tommy did.

Cade was happy just sitting and listening to Tommy befuddle Alistair and Nathaniel but he could see Dot was beginning to droop. She'd probably been out of bed way too long and needed to retire. He cleared his throat and looked over at Dot. "Miss Warner," he said, always calling her that in front of her family, "if you have a few minutes, I'd like to cover a few things with you. Shouldn't take long. Happy to meet you upstairs so you'll be more comfortable."

Alistair glanced at Dot. "Why don't I handle this, Aunt Dorothy? I don't think you should have to be bothered with decisions after a long day."

Dot looked at him and then at Cade. "How about the three of us meet tomorrow morning? It'd be nice to have you there, Alistair, but you're right, it has been a long day." Dot's hazel gaze met Cade's. "Is there anything urgent, Cade? Can we wait for the morning?"

Cade nodded. "Absolutely."

"Excellent." Dot slowly pushed herself up, using her fingertips on the table to gain her balance. "I'll see you boys here at six."

"Six?" Alistair spluttered. "In the morning?"

Dot's brow creased. "Ranch work begins early, Alistair. You know that."

"But, Aunt Dorothy, it's Sunday."

"Oh, I see. You're going to church."

Alistair flushed red. "No, not going to church. I just like to… sleep in."

"Well then, take advantage of your Sunday and sleep in." She looked at Cade. "I'll see you then in the morning."

MERRIBEE WALKED NEXT to Dot as Dot slowly climbed the stairs, leaning on the broad bannister. "I am tired," Dot confessed. "I should have taken a nap this afternoon instead of pouring over the books, but it's the end of the year, time to get everything in order."

"You don't have an accountant?"

"Oh, I do, but how can I trust him to get it right if I'm not familiar with my own numbers?"

They'd reached the top of the landing, and MerriBee took Dot's elbow and walked her down the hall to her bedroom suite. "You're pretty amazing, Miss Warner—"

"Call me Dot, please. You've seen me naked so it seems silly to stand on such formality."

MerriBee laughed aloud, her merriment echoing in the wood-paneled hall.

Dot gave her a sharp look. "Am I that funny?"

MerriBee blinked back tears and nodded, realizing that Dot's sharp tone hid a heart of gold. "You are hilarious."

Dot patted MerriBee's arm. "And you are just what we needed. I hope you can get Cade to open up, share his secrets with you. He deserves more out of this life, and I think you do, too."

AFTER DOT WAS in bed, MerriBee had planned on going to Cade's cabin to visit and say good night, but she was so tired from the day that she changed into her pajamas and just crawled beneath the sheets of her bed.

What were Cade's secrets? What did Dot mean by that? And of course Cade deserved more out of life. They all did.

A knock sounded on her door just as she was falling asleep. She left her bed, and went to the door. It was Cade.

"You didn't say good night," he said.

She gestured for him to come in, not wanting to attract the attention of any of the Jameses, and quietly closed the door behind him, and then turned on her bedside lamp, creating a cozy golden glow. "You were with Tommy and I was so tired."

He put a hand to her forehead. "Not coming down sick, are you?"

This was why she loved him. He was so practical, but also so kind. "No, Nurse Hunt, I'm fine. Just a little over-whelmed, I think. Not used to so many people in one house."

"Come stay at my place."

"That wouldn't be okay."

"Why? Because you're a virgin?"

She punched him lightly in the middle of his chest. "Hey! That's not to be thrown around lightly."

"I'm teasing you."

"I know. But still, it's weird at my age. I'm the first to admit it." She went and sat down on her bed, and patted the side of the mattress. "Come tell me about Tommy. Why did he come? Is everything okay? Everything seemed fine at dinner, but was that just an act?"

"He came here to meet me, and say welcome to the family."

"That was nice." She patted the mattress again. "Sit."

He shook his head. "If I sit down next to you, I'm going to kiss you senseless, and I will take liberties. My hands won't be able to not touch you. Now that I've discovered your lips, I think about your breasts—"

"Let's keep you standing then," she said crisply.

He laughed quietly and then his laughter faded. "Why haven't you remarried? You should have a husband and family that adore you. You shouldn't be alone, just giving and giving. You should be loved in return."

Her eyes suddenly smarted. "You know why. I've told you why."

"It doesn't make sense."

"Because you didn't know John."

"Explain it to me. I want to understand. I want to understand why this man made you give up all other men."

MerriBee heard the hardness in his voice, and the thread of anger. Cade was upset… with her. But why? "I've never questioned your love of the mountains, or the ranch—"

"I'm not questioning your commitment to nursing. I'm questioning why you've given up on love. You're too young, too beautiful, too generous, too alive."

"I've told you all this. John and I met and fell in love while his cancer was in remission. We broke up, and then he was back in my life, and we married." She paused, picturing John as he'd been when she'd first met him. Vibrant, handsome, thoughtful. Insightful.

He was someone who wasn't meant to die young. He wasn't someone who deserved to be in that bed. He was a former ski champion. He'd been an alternate for the US Olympic ski team. He was positive and strong, even while dying. John was always concerned about those around him. He wanted to know how things were on the ward. He wanted to know about other patients. He'd pray with her for them. He never asked for prayers for himself. He said he wasn't worried about himself, that he had a good life, a great life, that he couldn't ask for more.

"He was the kind of person I wanted to be," she said, forcing herself to continue. "He was very spiritual, and we shared the same values and beliefs."

"And his cancer?"

"It was bone cancer, advanced."

"You knew this when you married him?"

"Yes." MerriBee looked at Cade who was standing still, listening. "He didn't make it to our first anniversary, but we came close. He'd been doing well, and then he wasn't. In a matter of a week, he was just gone. I was curled up next to him on the bed when he stopped breathing. I knew he was gone from the stillness in the room." Her eyes burned and she drew an unsteady breath. "I swear I felt his spirit leave his body, and his spirit was exactly as I'd always known—golden. Glorious."

"And how can any mortal man compare to a saint?" Cade said after a taut silence.

His tone stung and she jerked her head back, looked up at him. "That's not fair."

"But true. You won't love anyone else because you loved him so much, and no one can measure up to Saint John."

"Stop it." She sat up tall. "You're being mean."

"I care for you, Bee, and I'd like a life with you, but I don't think I stand a chance. Do I?"

She didn't understand. What was he saying? "What does that mean? Are you proposing?"

"If I did, would you marry me? Would you live here and have a family with me? Because I think you need a husband and children. I think you need real people, living people, to fill your life and give you meaning."

She slid off the bed, faced him. "You seem to know an awful lot about what I need, when I have a feeling there is so much from your past that you haven't shared."

"I've told you about my childhood, I've told you about my mom's cancer, Jimmy, my sister, and the Wyatts."

"But that's not everything, is it? Dot says you have secrets, and that I'm supposed to get you to open up—"

"Why? So I can bare my soul for you to tell me that I'm not enough, and that you're needed in Marietta to tend the dying?"

"I don't know why you're being cruel, but it's not okay, and I'm not going to listen to it. If you care for me, if you love me, that's one thing, but if you're just going to take jabs at me because you're pissed off, then go."

"I don't want you to leave." He squared his shoulders, hooked his thumbs over his leather belt. "I know you have the Christmas baskets to deliver, but afterward, come back with me, let's spend Christmas here, and New Year's, and figure out if we have a future together, and if so, how we can make it work."

She liked him, and the ranch, and Dot, but she didn't feel secure here. She didn't belong here. "You mean, figure out a future on the Sundowner?"

"Yes."

MerriBee felt cold and overwhelmed, as well as sad. This wasn't what she wanted for her future. She loved him, but not this place, not this isolation, not Wyoming. Her home and heart were in Marietta. She loved Cade, but she needed her work. It was why she woke up in the morning, and what gave her meaning and purpose. "Cade, I don't know what to say."

"About spending Christmas here, or the future here?"

"I love my job, Cade, you know that."

"I love you, Bee. You must know that."

She looked away, the hollow sensation inside of her expanding, making her feel empty and colder. "I love you, too, but our lives are so different. What we want out of life is different. Even our beliefs are different. I need God, and my faith, and—" She broke off, glanced at him, and then shook her head. "You don't."

"Just because I don't have your faith, doesn't mean I

wouldn't want our children raised to believe, because if we had kids, I'd want them like you."

She squeezed her eyes shut, overwhelmed. His words were lovely, and the fact that he wanted to build a life with her touched her, deeply, but for a practical man, it was all incredibly impractical. Surely, he had to see that? "Do we have to decide this tonight?" she whispered, opening her eyes and looking at him. "Can we get those baskets delivered and then decide?"

"Of course." He started for the door.

"Cade," she said, stopping him. "Please don't think I don't care, because I do. I have loved the time we've spent together. I haven't been this happy in years."

"Me, too." He hesitated, jaw jutting, a fierce glint in his blue gaze. "But love isn't enough, and being happy isn't enough. Not for you."

"Cade."

"Just clarifying everything, Bee. I have a right to know where I stand."

"And we have to do this tonight?"

"No, not if you think you'll change your mind in the morning. If we'll have a different future in the morning." His gaze bored into hers. "Just be honest with me. Could you possibly give me a different answer tomorrow, or will it be more of the same I've heard tonight?"

She'd been cold earlier, and now she burned hot, her heart on fire. She couldn't, wouldn't, lie to him. She couldn't give him false hope. "No," she whispered. "I don't think I'll feel differently in the morning. I will love you— very much—but I'll still feel as if I've been called to my job, and to my work."

He gave her a long piercing look before he walked out the door, closing it firmly behind him.

CHAPTER TEN

CADE WAS AWAKE early the next morning and after coffee he dressed to head out for an early ride before the six o'clock meeting with Dot, which he suspected wasn't a meeting at all, but a test for Alistair. Regardless, Cade had things to do, and was eager to be outside, in the cold, thinking the sharp air would clear his head, calm his emotions.

He'd imagined a very different ending to what actually happened in Bee's room last night. He'd gone to say good night to her, spirits high, feeling hopeful... no, not just hopeful, but confident, certain that she felt the same way about him as he did about her. Their time together had made him believe she was falling in love with him. Kissing her, he'd felt passion, but also more. Tenderness. Happiness.

He had wanted her physically from the day they first met, but his desire had turned into wanting the best for her, needing to protect her, craving time with her. With her up at Dot's house, he missed her being close, missed all the little things—seeing her with her coffee in the morning, getting a glimpse of her reading, sitting with her on the couch watching a movie or show. He liked his cabin, but he'd like it more with her in it, sharing the space with him. There were two other bedrooms, besides his, and they'd be perfect for little people, and there was a corner in the cabin that needed a Christmas tree.

For the past few days, he'd given himself permission to dream, and he hadn't realized how many dreams he had. Now he needed to pull the dreams back and focus on reality. He'd lost sight of reality, had become impractical, his happiness making him too open, too hopeful.

Cade had just stepped outside his cabin when the door opened and Tommy appeared on the doorstep, dressed, but hair sticking up, and clearly not totally awake yet. "What's your plan?" he asked, smothering a yawn. "Anything I could help you with?"

"Was going to check one of the troughs in a pasture a mile from here, you're welcome to join me if you're up for a ride."

"Have a horse for me?"

"Yes. Go get some coffee and find a hat. You're going to need both to keep you warm."

The morning was clear, crisp and cold, temperatures in the low twenties with just a smattering of stars still visible in the lavender-gray sky. Cade had loved dawn from the moment he discovered that morning on the ranch was different from the mornings he knew growing up. His house had never been calm, and there had always been tension, as well as anxiety about what would happen next. He loved living in a place without a lot of roads, and cars, busses, and noise. There wasn't a train whistle to be heard or sirens to disturb the peace. Here, on his horse, watching the sun rise, he could see the world as an inherently good place. Here, close to nature, he could believe in God.

For a little bit there he'd even thought God had brought Bee into his life, but those were just more of his silly imaginings. He'd let down his guard and let himself feel, and now he just felt stupid. It'd be better, easier, when Bee left. Better for both of them, he suspected.

"When are you heading back to Paradise Valley?" Cade asked Tommy, who was riding next to him. "Not that I'm trying to rush you."

"It's Mom's birthday coming up—I never remember if it's the twenty-second or twenty-third—but I should get back, get some gifts, spend some time with her. She was disappointed that I'd only just arrived when I did some laundry, packed up, and headed here." He took a breath, grinned. "That's a long way of saying probably this morning, after something to eat. But I can also grab breakfast on the road."

"I'll feed you before I kick you out," Cade said.

"Thanks, bro, nice of you."

Cade's smile shifted, fading. "Can I ask a favor though?"

"Sure."

"Would you mind taking MerriBee with you? I promised

I'd get her home in time for her to deliver her Christmas baskets, and since you're heading that way…" He didn't finish the sentence, there was no need.

"No problem. It'd be nice to have company."

Cade was just about to add, *and no hitting on her*, but bit back the words at the last second because she wasn't his. MerriBee had made it clear she wanted something different from life than a future with him so there was no reason to scare off Tommy. Maybe Tommy would be a better fit for her. He lived in Paradise Valley, an easy drive from her hospital in Marietta. Maybe sending her home with him was exactly what he was supposed to do.

He didn't like the thought, though. It made his temper simmer and burn. He felt exhausted and furious, as well as utterly crushed, which wasn't how a man should ever feel. But he cared for her, so much, and now he was letting her go, and that made him crazy.

"Did you know Bee's husband, John Bradley?" he asked abruptly, looking at Tommy. "Not sure of his age. I figured he was Joe's age, maybe, possibly older."

"I didn't know him personally, but had heard about him. He was an Olympic skier, or an alternate to the Olympic team, I believe."

"He was a local guy then?"

"From what I remember, he was raised in Marietta before his family relocated to Colorado for the training facilities there."

They rode in silence for a bit, the horses moving easily across the white field.

"Does MerriBee know she's leaving with me this morning?" Tommy asked, as they reached a metal gate.

Cade dismounted to open the gate, swinging it wide enough for both horses to travel through. He shot Tommy a narrowed glance as he closed the gate behind them. "Why do you ask?"

"Because I wonder if you sending her back with me is part of your bad mood."

"Huh," Cade said, swinging back into the saddle. "Not in a bad mood."

"Nothing upset you last night?"

"No."

"You didn't come back from Miss Warner's and drink a six-pack by yourself?"

Cade shot Tommy another hard look. "I had four. You had two."

"And you said that you never drank more than two, because if you did, it reminded you of Jimmy and you never wanted to think of him, ever."

That much was true. Cade couldn't lose control because then he'd be Jimmy's boy, and he couldn't be that person, couldn't allow himself to be anything like his stepfather. "I was upset last night," he admitted. "I was disappointed."

Tommy looked at him, brow lifted.

Cade didn't want to talk, and yet... and yet, maybe he

did. Maybe Tommy wouldn't be a bad person to talk to. He didn't work with him, or answer to him. He wasn't a ranch employee, wouldn't gossip to anyone he knew, nor did Tommy strike Cade as someone who'd get up in his face. "I thought things were heading in a certain direction with Bee, but I thought wrong. We're not on the same page, and it caught me off guard." He shrugged dismissively, but on the inside his chest was tight, his lungs aching with each breath. "Better to know now, though."

"You love her?"

Cade frowned, irritated. "I don't throw that word around loosely, but yes, I do."

"Then give her space and some time. She might come around."

Cade's hurt blazed into anger. "I'm not interested in someone who needs to 'come around.' If she doesn't feel the way I do, I'd rather just cut my losses now, save myself a whole lot of heartache."

Tommy shot him a rueful look. "It's too late for that. You'll have heartache, either way."

"But at least this way, I won't feel stupid and vulnerable with my heart out there. I had enough of that growing up. Don't need more of that now."

"I respect that."

Reaching the trough, Cade broke the layer of ice on top, spotted a section of the fence that was sagging and walked over to check it out. Tommy had dismounted and was walking next to him. "Beautiful place here," he said, gaze skimming the white mountain peaks.

"Peaceful," Cade answered, before adding, "well, not as peaceful in summer when the guests come, but the rest of the time, it's what I think heaven must be like. You know, God's country."

"I'm looking for a place like that myself."

"Not going to live on the Wyatt ranch?"

"Too many Wyatts for me, and Sophie's pregnant again. The Wyatt ranch is their home. I need to figure out where I'll be. I've got the money to invest, but haven't found the place."

"Hoping to stay close to your family?"

"Ideally, yes. Both Mom and Granddad are getting older, and I know they like having us around. I've always been extra close with Mom, maybe because I'm the youngest. I'd hate to move too far and not see her much. As it is, I'm on the road most of the time. But the rodeo's been good to me, and I have good contracts and sponsors. I get more beat up every year, but I can't walk away yet."

Cade smiled at Tommy, his cousin. How crazy it was to have cousins. All these years without any family and now there was a whole mess of Wyatts over in Montana that were related to him. "Just make sure you walk away," Cade said, aware of the immense dangers in the Wyatt family's sport, "while you can walk away."

❧

MERRIBEE COULDN'T BELIEVE that she had just been packed up and sent away, as if a rebellious child in disgrace. She barely had time to say goodbye to Dot, before she was hustled down the stairs while Cade had carried her things to Tommy's truck and sent on her way.

There had been no conversation with Cade this morning. There had been no chance to talk things through. She'd slept terribly last night, crying into her pillow, overwhelmed and confused. She'd woken and felt a desperate need for information, and clarity, but no, for Cade it was all done. He was so black and white. It was his way or no way, and now, it was over.

Thank goodness Tommy seemed to understand that she was pretty much devastated. He turned the radio on and didn't try to make conversation. She stared sightlessly out the window, an impossibly large lump in her throat, tears in her eyes. He stopped for gas north of Sheridan and then went through a Starbucks drive through, picking up coffees for the ride home. The mocha was exactly what she needed. Well, it helped for a bit, but then the tears started again, and she kept swiping hem away, hoping Tommy wouldn't see.

"You okay, MerriBee?" he asked, an hour outside Billings.

She nodded and struggled to smile. "I'm good." And yet the tears burned hotter and fell faster. She kept wiping them away, even as she smiled. "Not sure why I am crying. Just probably overtired."

"I gather this abrupt departure wasn't at your request?"

"No, but if this is what Cade wants…" She shrugged. "Then I guess this is the best way."

"He told me a little bit about what happened last night. Want to tell me your side of it?" He glanced at her. "Not trying to be pushy, but didn't know if talking about it would help at all, and we do have three more hours of driving ahead of us."

"I don't even know what happened last night." She reached up and used her knuckles to dry beneath her eyes. "He came upstairs to say good night, and then, and then… we were through." She laughed, and sniffed. "I need a tissue. You don't have anything, do you?"

"Check the glove box. There should be some paper napkins in there."

He was right, and she took out several and blew her nose, wiped her eyes dry, and blew her nose one more time. "He and I have never once talked about marriage. We never talked about love. We never talked about kids. Well, not true, I said that I probably would never have kids. I think that's what I said. But there were no discussions about us together. And then last night he comes in and says it was time we made some decisions." She looked at Tommy, baffled. "I didn't see any of that coming. There was no setup. There was nothing to indicate that he was going to propose—"

"He proposed?"

"No. There was no formal proposal. He said *if* he proposed, would I move to Wyoming?" She still couldn't believe it. "*If* he proposed. Who says it like that? Who puts someone on the spot like that? What we needed were conversations that lead up to that conversation. Explored our ideas for the future, talk about what we both wanted, right?"

Tommy was silent for a long minute. He turned on his signal, took the exit that would let them merge onto the next highway. "Maybe Cade thought you had." Tommy looked at her, curious. "Did he ever say anything about his future on the Sundowner Ranch? Did he ever talk about wanting to leave it?"

"No, he doesn't want to leave. He loves that ranch. He loves Dot, and he's not going to leave her... not while she's alive. After she's gone, that might be a different story."

Tommy changed lanes, merging into the fastest lane. "And you're committed to Marietta."

"If I moved to Cade, I would have to give up my work, and my work means everything to me."

"So, in short, more than Cade?"

She winced. "You don't need to put it like that."

"But that is what you are saying."

"Isn't it the same for him?" She looked at Tommy, angry. "There is property all throughout Montana. There are ranchers everywhere. Why couldn't he take a job on another ranch in Paradise Valley? Why couldn't he buy some property of his own in Paradise Valley? We could also live up near

Livingston. We could move toward Bozeman. There's a huge hospital there, I could find lots of work there. But for me to leave my work, it doesn't make sense. I would have nothing to do on the ranch."

"Seems like you do have your answer."

"But you feel sorry for Cade."

"I feel sorry for both of you," he corrected, before turning the radio back up.

MerriBee got her phone out, and scanned her email, and then scrolled through the news headlines, and read anything that would keep her busy. She didn't want to think about Cade and didn't want to feel guilty. There was no reason for her to feel guilty. She'd done nothing wrong. It didn't seem fair that she'd been turned into the villain, either.

She could see how she'd be the villain if she'd ever led Cade on. But she'd never talked about marriage with him, and yes, she'd mentioned maybe having kids, but she'd never said *with him*. And yes, she knew he was attracted to her, but she'd had no idea he was serious about her. He hadn't ever said a word.

He'd barely opened up.

He'd shared only the most basic things with her, and then, it was after she'd pushed and prodded. How could she see a future with someone who didn't talk to her? Who didn't share what he was thinking, or feeling? John had been an incredible communicator. John had been open and warm. Giving.

Cade was giving, and Cade could be warm, but he didn't let her in, and she couldn't imagine a life with someone who didn't talk about the big things... the important things. Life was full of challenges. Life was full of disappointments. If you couldn't talk to each other during the hard times, what kind of relationship was that?

She drew a slow, deep breath as she put away her phone. Reading anything in the car made her queasy. She needed to stop looking down. As it was, she felt a headache coming on. The headache she could do something about, pop a couple painkillers and that would make it go away. The heartache, that was different. There was nothing she could take for that.

CADE RARELY FORGOT important things, like meetings with his boss, but that morning wasn't typical, and in his desire to settle his emotions, he'd focused on only one thing after the dawn ride with Tommy—get MerriBee back to Marietta where she belonged. It wasn't until he got a call requesting his presence up at the big house that he remembered what he'd forgotten—Dot.

She was in the library when he arrived, and Emma was sitting with her, in front of the gas fireplace in a pair of winged leather chairs, both having coffee and something warm and mouthwatering, smelling of butter and sugar Emma must have just baked. But when he stepped into the room, Emma rose, gave him a sharp look, and walked out.

No smile, no good morning, nothing.

He crossed to the armchair just vacated and sat down. "I forgot our meeting. I'm sorry."

Dot lifted her dainty coffee cup and sipped it. "You had other things on your mind," she said.

He knew what she was referencing. He'd been in the upstairs hall when Bee had gone to Dot's bedroom to say goodbye. When it seemed as if the two were going to get into a conversation, he'd interrupted, reminding MerriBee that Tommy was in the truck, waiting. It wasn't the total truth. Tommy was by the truck waiting, but still, there was no reason to drag out the goodbyes. They weren't easy for anyone.

"I didn't know she was leaving today, never mind so early," Dot added, looking at him with that steady gaze of hers, a gaze that often saw far too much. "She hadn't mentioned anything the night before about departing."

If it was anyone else, Cade would have walked out. He didn't want to have this conversation, and didn't like the confrontational tone—subtle as it was. "She needed to get back to Marietta for her annual Christmas project. She organizes and delivers baskets to families in need in the community and I'd promised to get her back, but since Tommy was heading that way today, it made sense to just get her a ride now." Cade stopped talking, realizing he was practically babbling. He could see from Dot's expression that she thought so, too.

"She told me about her baskets. She has a giving heart, doesn't she?"

Cade fought his temper. Yes, Bee had a giving heart... and loved to be giving for others, strangers. People who weren't him. He gritted his jaw, smashed his hurt. It stung, being rejected like this. It made him angry and want to bash things, break things. "Don't provoke me, Dot. Not today. I can't cope—"

"What did she do to hurt you?"

Cade's chest burned, his heart ached. Everything inside of him felt raw. Even his skin hurt, nerves sensitive. "She didn't."

"She did."

He looked away, stared at the portrait of her grandfather hanging above the fireplace. He'd been a decorated colonel in the Civil War, and after the war, after he'd recovered from losing part of his leg, amputated after a wound wouldn't heal, had come west and bought land in the Big Horn Mountains. The Warners had been here ever since. If Dot had had children, there would have been four generations of Warners born and raised here. But she hadn't and so the ranch would pass to others.

The library was so quiet and for a moment Cade forgot where he was, and what was being discussed, and then voices sounded in the hall, voices of Dot's family just now heading to breakfast. "I asked her if she'd be willing to come live here with me." Cade forced himself to meet Dot's eyes. "She said no."

Dot carefully set her cup on the side table. "I didn't realize you'd bought a ring. You should have come to me. I would have given you a family piece. I have all my mother's jewelry—"

"I didn't have a ring, and I wouldn't have accepted one from you, either."

High-pitched barking could be heard from the dining room. The dogs were either chasing each other around the table, or they were up on the table. Hard to know.

Her thin sloped shoulders shrugged. "My mother's jewelry was elegant and classic, and would have suited your Bee."

Again his temper surged. He beat it back, checked his tone. "She's not my Bee anymore."

"Ah, I see." Dot folded her hands in her lap, hazel gaze narrowed, thoughtful. "I'm sorry."

But she didn't sound sorry, she sounded as if she pitied him, and there was a difference.

"There will be other girls," Dot added, gesturing with one wrinkled hand. "There are plenty of fish in the sea."

He rose. "Now you're just being patronizing."

She struggled to stand and when he moved to help her she gave another impatient gesture.

Once she was on her feet, standing straight, she looked him in the eye. "My grandfather left my grandmother and the children behind to fight in a war to preserve this country. He returned wounded, and spent another year fighting for his life. He came out west to fight for a new life, something away from the city chaos so that his family could have space. Opportunity. My father raised four children, and I was the only one who lived to twenty-five. I have fought to keep this land in the family, running a ranch when men didn't work with women, and men didn't want to answer to a woman. You've had your battles, too, Cade. Your life hasn't been easy, but that should make you just fight harder, not surrender. We Warners never surrender, and you might not have my DNA, but I've tried to teach you the things I would have taught my son. Think like a Warner, not a Hunt or an O'Connell."

THE LAST HOUR of the drive had felt endless. MerriBee couldn't get comfortable, her legs aching, her body stiff. She was so relieved when Tommy pulled up in front of her house. He carried her things to her doorstep, gave her a quick hug goodbye, and waited for MerriBee to unlock the front door before returning to his truck. Once he was gone, she went in. The house was freezing. MerriBee turned the heater on, flipped on lights, and then finally, turned on the living room's Christmas tree lights. They were on a timer and would have come on late afternoon, but she needed the cheer now.

She felt terrible. Her head was still throbbing, and her heart felt even worse.

She didn't even know what had happened. She should have refused to leave when he pointed her to the door. There was no reason Tommy couldn't have waited a half hour, or an hour. No reason she had to even leave that day. Maybe things wouldn't have played out differently, but at least she wouldn't have felt so shaken. The goodbye had been so abrupt, the dismissal by Cade nothing short of callous. It had felt unnecessarily cruel.

Why not talk to her?

Why not give it—her—some time?

But no, she'd hurt him, and so he'd lashed out, hurting her in return. Cade, the wounded grizzly bear.

Just thinking his name made her want to start crying again. So she wouldn't think of him. She'd do anything and everything but think of him.

MerriBee went through the house, plugging in all the Christmas trees, and turning on all the music boxes—the four bears on a frozen lake—more bears!—the pair of angels heralding on their golden trumpets, the little Clara in her jewel box of a ballroom. She let all the music boxes play at once, a cacophony of sound, not at all pleasing, but it was loud and sharp, and suited her mood.

She hadn't grown up in a family that did Christmas in a big way. There had been no extravagant decorations, no outdoor light parade. They'd had a modest-sized tree, and a modest artificial wreath, a wreath that was recycled and hung on the front door every year. But John had loved Christmas with all the trimmings. He'd loved the lights and the carols, the stories and the movies. He wanted a fire in the hearth, and the scent of cranberry and cinnamon candles burning. And so she gave him the Christmas he deserved in their last few weeks together, and every year since, she recreated the Christmas magic. In honor of John, whose faith never wavered, not even as he died.

Her faith, well, she'd need that more than ever now, as she felt no peace about the ending with Cade, felt no calm or confidence that she was on the right path. Maybe it was too soon to feel peace. Maybe she had to grieve before the calm came, but peace would come, not in the world, but in Him.

After hours of sitting it felt good to move. She unpacked her bag, did some laundry, ran a small load of dishes. The painkillers she took didn't help her head yet, and every time she swallowed, her throat hurt. But with a good night's rest, some hot honey tea, and one of her frozen homemade soups for dinner, she should feel better in the morning.

But the next morning, MerriBee felt worse. Her throat was so sore now she didn't want to swallow. She ached all over, and just getting out of bed to use the bathroom made her feel like a cement truck had rolled over her. Washing her hands, she looked at the cast on her left hand, more than ready to get it off. It had been a hard month. Between crashing into her front steps, getting her heart mashed up, and now coming down with the flu, this wasn't a festive December.

Although, it wasn't all bad, she conceded, drying her hands. The time with Cade had been special, more than special. He'd been terrible and then wonderful, and now terrible again, but he'd also been her friend, and her champion, and she was grateful for that.

She'd also gotten to meet Dorothy Warner, an impressive woman who was a legend in the West. Being able to stay in her gorgeous, historic home had been amazing. The house was filled with an irreplaceable art collection, both paintings and sculpture. And then she'd met the James family, and had firsthand experience with the little dogs, including Mitsy the Pekingese who couldn't figure out when and where to go to the bathroom.

Flicking on lights, MerriBee dragged herself downstairs to make coffee. Her head felt terrible. The coffee tasted different, strangely bitter. She added more sugar, more milk, but it didn't help. Miserable, she leaned against the counter, joints aching, head spinning. She didn't want coffee. She just wanted to go back to bed.

MerriBee slept off and on throughout the day, waking up at some point early afternoon, drenched in sweat. She stumbled to the bathroom, took her temperature, 101.8.

Not the end of the world for an adult, but she didn't want it to get much higher. She took something for the fever, washed it down with as much water as she could, considering her swollen throat, and then climbed back into bed, scooting to the side of the sheets that weren't damp.

Closing her eyes, it crossed her mind, that it would have been nice if Cade was here. She didn't want to miss him, and she didn't want to need him, but he'd been such good company earlier in the month. He'd made everything easier. Better. He'd made her realize what it was like having a partner, someone else to help, someone to take over so you didn't have to do everything yourself.

She pressed her face into her pillow.

She wasn't crying, she simply wasn't feeling good. If tears were falling, she wasn't crying for Cade, or crying because everything had ended so abruptly. She just felt off and a little bit lonely. Because no one *really* wanted to be alone their whole life. No one really *wanted* to grow old alone. For a brief period of time, she'd had someone who wanted her, someone who said he loved her, but how could God bring someone into her life who didn't fit into the plan?

CHAPTER ELEVEN

C ADE DIDN'T NEED anyone telling him who he was, or who he was supposed to be. Not even Dot.

Especially Dot.

She hadn't lived his life. She hadn't been raised with addiction, abuse, and lies. She'd never known what it was to be nothing, to be no one. She'd never had so little self-respect that she'd legally changed her name, desperate for a fresh start.

But she was right about one thing. He wasn't an O'Connell, and he wasn't a dirty fighter. He regretted sending Bee away so abruptly. He'd been rough. Unkind. It was immature of him. If he could, he would have changed the way their goodbyes were said. He would have given her a hug, held her close one last time, and wished her well. Because he wanted the best for her, he did. And he would have cherished that last hug, that last feel of her in his arms, the smell of her, the softness of her cheek against his chest.

Every day he regretted the harsh goodbye a bit more. All Tuesday he thought of her, and he checked his phone repeatedly, hoping she'd maybe text, give him an opening to reach out to her. But she didn't text or call. Tuesday night, Cade called Tommy and asked about the drive home on Sunday.

Tommy said it had been fine. No problems, no scenes. "I mean, of course she was sad," he added. "She cried. But she's a strong woman. She'll be fine."

Cade hung up and folded his arms across his chest, hands forming fists. The issue wasn't her being strong. The issue wasn't her being fine.

The issue was him being an ass. He'd been cruel. Unkind.

He closed his eyes, frustrated with himself. Every time he thought he was finally a man, he did something stupid, proved that he wasn't who he wanted to be yet.

And this had nothing to do with what Dot had said on Sunday. This was his truth. This was his life and the dreams he had.

If he wanted to be better than Jimmy then he had to act differently than Jimmy.

He grabbed his phone and punched in Bee's number and then hesitated. What would he say? *I'm sorry.* Was that enough? Was that what she needed to hear?

Was that all he needed to say?

He put his phone in his pocket, but he felt haunted all day. He talked to Willis that evening, gave him a note for Dot explaining his absence, and woke up before dawn on Wednesday to head to Montana.

He'd thought the early start would get him to Marietta by ten, but road work on one stretch of the highway, and then just west of Billings there was a four-car pileup that impacted all lanes, and it ended up being one of those days where you did more waiting than driving. It was about one when Cade pulled up in front of the red Christmas house on Bramble Lane. Two newspapers still lay wrapped in plastic on the walkway. One of the plastic candy canes lining the walk was on its side, frost glittering across its red and white stripes. He fixed the candy cane, pressing it back into the ground and gathered the newspapers before knocking on the front door.

He waited, but there was no answer. He tried the door. It was locked. He knocked again, waited and when she still didn't come, Cade went to the kitchen window and peeked in. The kitchen was dark. The house was dark. He'd think she was out but her car was here, in the driveway, up against the nonfunctioning garage door.

Cade called her. She finally answered on the sixth or seventh ring. She sounded out of it. "Cade?"

"Yeah, Bee. I'm downstairs. Can you let me in?"

He could hear her moving, sheets rustling. "You're where?" she asked, sounding dazed.

"Here. Outside." He waited, trying to picture her. "Are you still in bed?"

"I don't feel so good."

"What's wrong?" he asked.

"Sick. You don't want it."

"How long have you been sick?"

More covers rustling. "Sunday? Now go away because I'm not going to expose you to this."

"Bee, it's Wednesday. What's happening with your baskets? Do you have them all together? You deliver them tomorrow."

"What day is it?"

"*Wednesday.* The twenty-second. I thought you had to pick up the hams and turkeys—"

"It can't be the twenty-second already. What time is it?"

"One."

She hung up abruptly. He stood there not sure if she'd fainted or was on her way down. Either way, he'd give her to the count of ten before he broke in. *One, two, three, four.*

He glanced up at the house, thought about the window he'd go through. Perhaps one in the bedroom in the back.

Five, six, seven.

Yes, the bedroom window. He started heading to the gate. *Eight, nine—*

The front door swung open. He turned around. *Ten.*

She stood on the doorstep, a robe hanging from her shoulders, the tie dragging on the ground. Her long red hair was a tangled mess, and her face so pale he could see purple crescents beneath her eyes. "You look dreadful," he said, going to her.

She glared at him. "And you look hot," she said. "Not as

in feverish, but sexy, which isn't right considering how mean you are."

The corner of his mouth lifted. He felt a pang in his chest. So fierce, so feisty, so his... even if she didn't want to be his. He could love her even if she didn't want the same things he did. He could love her even if they didn't have the same future. "I'm sorry. I didn't handle your rejection well."

"Is that why you're here?"

He heard something in her voice, disappointment maybe, and felt another pang. She was hoping he'd want what she wanted. She was hoping he could see a life for them here. "And to help with those baskets," he said, because they had been in the back of his mind, bugging him. He'd told her he would help and then he'd dropped out of the picture. Not cool of him. Not the kind of man he wanted to be. It's not as if he needed to be a hero, but he should at least have some integrity. "I'd offered my help, remember?"

"Things changed."

He had nothing to say to that, and she walked her back into the house and closed the door. "Do you have a fever?"

"It's a little better today."

"Headache?"

"Yes."

"Sore throat?"

"Not so bad."

"Body aches?" he asked, drawing her robe over her shoulders, and then tying the sash around her waist.

"Better with pain meds."

"Have you eaten lately?"

"Some canned soup…" She paused, frowned. "Yesterday? A piece of toast today."

"Not hungry?"

"No energy."

He swung her up in his arms and started for the stairs. "I'll get you sick," she said, averting her head.

"Then don't talk."

He felt her ribs lift with muffled laughter and some of the ache in his chest eased. He was here, and she'd be okay.

But once she was back in her bed she didn't lie down. "I can't rest," she said. "There's too much to do."

"I've got it."

"No—"

"I know what needs to be done. I've seen all your lists in the garage of everything that needs to be picked up, as well as from where, and when—"

"Which is today. Fifteen hams, twenty-two turkeys, twenty-four pies—"

"Twenty-four dozen rolls, I know. Most families get a ham or a turkey, but there are a few that get both."

"Yes." She looked up at him, eyes wide. "Many of those businesses close in just a few hours. The turkeys come from Livingston. Half of the pies come from the diner, and the others from a baker on the edge of town."

"It's in your notes."

"Cade, this is something that takes all day."

"Depends on how one approaches it. Let me go study your lists—"

"Hurry!"

"And I'll come up with a plan."

"There's no time to waste."

He laughed. "Calm down, Red. I've got this."

IF CADE HAD learned anything from running a big ranch, it was that you couldn't do it on your own, so the first thing he did, after heading to the garage to review Bee's lists, was call Tommy. "I'm here at Bee's," he said. "She's sick, and needs help to finishing getting her baskets together—"

"I'm in," Tommy said, before Cade could even make the request. "I'm on my way."

"I'll text you the information on the turkeys and hams. If you could pick those up, I'll hit the bakery and diner, for the rolls and pies, and then pick up the gingerbread cookies."

"Is that all MerriBee needs?"

"She's missing some gift cards—"

"Let me know how many and the amounts. I can ask Sam to get those. He's in town with Joe now."

"Are you sure?"

"*Yes.*"

Cade remembered the weather report for Wyoming. The Big Horn Mountains were going to be hit by a storm. He didn't know if Paradise Valley would get hit or be protected. "Have you heard anything weather-wise?"

"Snow's coming. Could be a lot."

"I heard the same. I think we should get the baskets delivered tomorrow as early as possible." Cade paused. "If you're willing to help me deliver."

"I know the area better than you. Makes sense to tackle the deliveries together. Leaving now. I'll see you at Merri-Bee's soon."

MUSIC WAS COMING from downstairs. Voices. Laughter. MerriBee turned her head and blinked into her pillow, groggily trying to place all the different sounds. She had no idea how long she'd been asleep but, looking out her window, it was dark and the strings of colored lights outlining the roof and windows glowed brightly.

She sat up, grabbed her robe, and used her fingers to comb her hair into a ponytail and slowly went down the stairs, trying to peek into the living room and kitchen without having to reveal herself. Unfortunately, she was seen and Sophie let out a cry of welcome, and then Tommy and Cade appeared from the garage and Sam and Joe emerged from the kitchen, with Sam eating a slice of pizza.

MerriBee held a hand up to stop them. "You don't want my germs."

"True," Tommy agreed, "but glad you're awake so you

can go over everything and make sure we have it right for the morning."

"We're going to divide up the baskets," Cade said. "Tommy and I will take half, and then Joe and Sam will deliver the other half, focusing on the families in the valley."

"Those aren't baskets," Sophie said. "They're baskets and boxes and bags. You have so much food."

MerriBee sat down on a stair. "Some of the families are big."

"We saw that," Sophie said. "And we picked up the missing gift cards. Everything is ready and wrapped. Just waiting to be delivered."

"How?" MerriBee said, peeking at everyone through the railing.

"Cade called me," Tommy said. "I called the family. Here we are."

MerriBee was humbled. "Thank you. I feel guilty needing so much help."

"Don't," Cade said. "You know, Joan of Arc didn't fight alone. She had soldiers. And now you have some, too. We're all here for you."

MerriBee blinked back tears. "I hate dragging others into my projects."

"We all volunteered, Bee," he answered. "We all wanted to give, do our part. After all, it's almost Christmas. Let us have our Christmas joy."

Her eyes burned, and she drew a rough breath. "Cade

Hunt, did you just use the word Christmas and joy in the same sentence?"

His lips curved. "I think I did. Maybe the whole festive thing is growing on me."

"Oh, I love this carol!" Sophie cried, dancing back into the living room to turn the music up.

Joe followed his wife into the living room and Sam disappeared and returned with a slice of pizza on a paper napkin. "From Rocco's," he said, passing the pizza slice to her, over the top of the bannister.

She looked at the pizza, saw the pineapple and smiled. Her favorite kind. She then looked at Cade who was back in conversation with Tommy, and her chest felt tender.

Cade had come through for her again.

But of course he had. He was loyal and loving. Protective, honest, and reliable. He was pretty much perfect— except his life was four and a half hours away, and it wasn't an easy drive, not in winter, not with the wind and ice and frequent whiteouts. But she wouldn't think of that tonight. She'd just be grateful and count her blessings.

CADE WAS BACK in the train room.

Nothing had changed, and yet everything had changed. He woke in the night and something drew his attention to the window. Pushing aside the blinds he looked out. Snow was falling, and from the look of it, had been falling for a long time. It was good they'd divided the baskets up. The roads would be challenging tomorrow.

He went back to bed, but checked that his alarm was set. Tomorrow would be a big day. He didn't want to risk oversleeping.

Four hours later he was up, dressed, and downstairs making coffee. While he waited for it to finish brewing, he sent a text to Tommy to see how the conditions were on their mountain as it was still snowing in town.

Tommy called him back. "Going to have to plow the road before I can meet you. It's going to take a while."

"Not a problem. I'll start with those in town and work my way to you."

"Smart. But, uh, Cade?"

"Yeah?"

"You are going to wait until the sun's up, aren't you? Not everyone keeps your hours."

Smiling crookedly, Cade hung up and poured himself coffee. He liked Tommy. He was easygoing and funny, someone he'd want to hang out with, someone he could see becoming a really good friend. Joe and Sam showing up yesterday had also helped heal the rift. They'd all agreed to come together on MerriBee's behalf, as well as focus on things that were important—Granddad and Christmas. Before Joe and Sophie left last night, they'd invited him to join them for Summer's birthday dinner tomorrow evening, but Cade had declined, not wanting to intrude on their family time.

For the next hour Cade continued to monitor the weather. The snow kept tumbling down, and the wind blew hard, sending the white stuff sideways, making it less than ideal driving conditions, but he'd manage. With or without Tommy. There was no way he'd let Bee down or the families relying on her to make Christmas special.

She appeared at seven, hair wet, dressed in leggings and an oversized sweater.

"You're up," he said.

"Feeling almost human."

"Want coffee?"

"Yes, please."

"Go sit by the fire," he directed. "I'll bring the coffee to you."

She did, because although she was better than yesterday, she'd need a day or so to fully recover. But from her chair in the living room she could see the snow coming down, and it was thick, so thick, she couldn't see anything beyond the window.

MerriBee used her phone to check the local weather and then wished she hadn't.

Cade brought her coffee and cinnamon toast and she smiled at him, touched. "My mom used to make cinnamon toast for me when I was sick. But it didn't have quite this much sugar."

"It's better with a lot of butter, cinnamon and sugar."

"Thank you."

"Of course." He held his hands out to the fire, warming them.

"No. Thank you. For everything."

He nodded, smiled at her. "Now we just have to get those baskets delivered."

She glanced out the window again. "It's almost a blizzard."

"If the wind blows any harder, it will be."

"How are you going to be able to drive?"

He shrugged. "I've driven in worse."

"Cade, it's dangerous."

"It'd be easier without the storm, but twenty-four families are looking forward to these baskets, twenty-four families with children. Children love Christmas. We will not disappoint them."

She hesitated. "I'm not running a fever anymore—"

"I'm not going to let you do it."

"But what if we did some together? I know the local families. I know where they live. We could get a lot done quickly if we worked together."

"You can't go out in this weather. It's freezing and it's coming down hard."

"What if I stayed in the truck? What if I stayed where it was warm? You could take the basket and things to the door?"

He said nothing for a moment and then sighed. "You

have an answer for everything."

"You've taught me that many hands make light work."

"Huh." He gave her a long look and then shook his head. "Make sure your hair is dry, and you're bundled up. I'll start loading the truck with the baskets for those in Crawford County. Hopefully once we're done, Tommy will be free and he and I can tackle Park County next."

THEY WEREN'T ABLE to deliver everything in one day. Eighteen baskets made it to eighteen grateful families, but the heavy snow meant they couldn't make it up and down all the unplowed mountain roads. As it grew dark, Tommy said he had to head back as it was his mom's birthday and he couldn't miss it. Cade understood. But that meant there were still six baskets to deliver the morning of the twenty-fourth.

Cade returned to Marietta and filled MerriBee in. She understood how difficult it was in the challenging conditions and focused on what had been accomplished—eighteen baskets had found homes.

"I'll get the rest delivered tomorrow, I promise," he assured her.

"I'm not worried. I have full confidence in you."

Cade met Tommy up at the Wyatt ranch at eight on Christmas Eve morning. Tommy wasn't quite ready and Billy, who'd just arrived from Utah with his family, greeted

Cade, and invited him in for a cup of coffee while Tommy finished dressing.

Billy, who'd been told all about Cade, was interested in hearing about the DNA test and results, as well as the website that had linked them. "It was my wife's doing," Billy said. "She'd wanted to establish paternity for Beck, and so I took a test, but I didn't know she'd uploaded the information anywhere. Or, maybe that was a different test. She was trying to build out a family tree for our baby, family trees and ancestry being big where we live in Utah."

"Without that test, I would have never known who my dad was, so thank you," Cade said.

"Did it change anything?" Billy asked, curious. "Do you feel different?"

"I still need to find my sister, but at least I now know that my biological father was a good man, and he came from a solid, loving family. That helps a lot. It's reassuring. Gives me hope that maybe I won't be a disaster as a dad." Cade pictured Jimmy, but the image of Jimmy was chased away by Melvin Wyatt coming through the kitchen door. His boots dusted in snow. The hem of his jeans damp.

"Morning boys," Melvin said, taking off his hat, and running fingers through his still thick white hair. "It's almost Christmas."

"Yes, it is," Cade agreed, and for the first time in forever, he was looking forward to Christmas, not for the presents, or the food, but rather the spirit of the season. He was grateful to have answers, grateful for this family, and grateful for his Bee, whether or not they ended up together.

IN THE END, they were one basket short. But it wasn't because MerriBee had miscounted. It was because late midafternoon, while delivering their last basket, they learned about a family in desperate need of help. It was during that last delivery, the Johnsons told them about a neighbor down the road, maybe a half mile down the road, set back in the woods, and the family was struggling, they were hungry and without electricity.

Tommy and Cade followed the directions and found the family, and what the Johnsons told them was true. There was virtually no food in the cupboards. There was no heat other than a meager fire in the fireplace, most of their wood wet from the recent storms.

The dad had been hurt in a logging accident a year ago and was still bedbound. The mom cleaned houses when she could, but with her kids sick, and their only vehicle out of commission due to a failed transmission, the family was struggling, and suffering.

They left the small house and climbed into Tommy's truck. Tommy started the engine. He looked at Cade. "That was rough," he said quietly.

"I've seen a lot of poverty, but that's bad," Cade agreed.

Tommy shifted into drive. "How is it that this family has

flown under the radar? How is it that no one knew how bad they were, except another struggling neighbor?"

Cade gave his head a slight shake. There were times his family had very little. And it wasn't something you ever advertised. "Even poor people are proud. No one wants to be looked down upon."

"And MerriBee's baskets are gone," Tommy said.

"We gave everything away." Cade knew that when MerriBee found out about this family, she'd be devastated. She'd want to do something, but at three in the afternoon on one of the shortest days of the year, there wasn't going to be sunlight much longer, and the snow would be falling again soon. "I wish we'd kept some things back. Giving them something would be better than nothing."

Tommy's huge four-by-four handled the narrow road, but it hadn't been plowed in weeks and it was as slow going out, as it had been going in. "I have an idea. It's a little bit crazy but we could pull it off."

"As long as it leaves MerriBee out of it. She's exhausted."

"She's not going to have to do anything. This isn't MerriBee's job. This is a Wyatt job." Tommy glanced at Cade. "It's a job for us, and I'm going to need your help, whether you like it or not."

Cade smiled grimly. "Put like that, how can I refuse?"

Tommy laughed. "You remind me more of my brother Sam than my brother Sam."

"And everyone tells me that Sam is an awful lot like your

uncle Sam."

"Yeah, your dad."

Cade just sat there with the words filling him, giving him a sense of calm, a sense of peace. It was a quiet drive to the Wyatt ranch. Tommy concentrated on the roads, country Christmas carols playing softly on the radio. Cade was glad Tommy knew the back roads well, because the thick snow blanketed signs and turns, changing the look of landmarks.

But then they were finally back at the Wyatt ranch and all the Wyatts had arrived, with the brothers and their wives and kids gathering in the kitchen, wanting to hear how the deliveries went. Tommy made sure his mother was seated at the kitchen table before telling them about the last family they saw.

Granddad gave Cade a quick hug before taking a position by the stove. The kitchen was crowded, but it felt comfortable, and Cade felt at ease, as if he was welcomed, as if he belonged. Maybe he did belong. Maybe these were his people.

Tommy cleared his throat. "I know it's Christmas Eve, and we're supposed to have dinner in just a couple hours, but we discovered a family that is in trouble. They have no heat, they have no food, they have young children. The conditions were terrible."

"We'd run out of MerriBee's baskets," Cade said. "The family wasn't on her list, but another family told us about them, and we went to check on them, and it was worse than we expected."

Tommy scuffed his boot. "I've never seen such hungry little people ever before. They literally looked like they were starving." He looked around the room, at his mom, grandfather and brothers. "We have to do something. We have so much, and they have nothing."

"How is it that they haven't gotten help from the county?" Joe asked.

Tommy shook his head. "I don't know, but they've been overlooked, and they need help. They need *us*."

"Agreed," Summer said quietly. "There's just no way we can have our big dinner, and then our big Christmas morning, and open gifts in a nice warm house while a family is starving, and freezing, just a couple miles from here."

Tommy's head tipped. "That's exactly how I feel, Mom. I don't get emotional about very many things, but that was rough. I can't stop thinking about those kids."

"This is divine intervention," Melvin said. "You were meant to go there today. Now we just need to do our part."

"What are the ages of the kids?" Sophie asked.

Tommy glanced at Cade. "What do you think?"

"They were young," Cade answered. "The oldest was probably nine or ten—" He broke off, frowned. "Well, she might have been older, but she was awfully small."

"She was trying hard to take care of the others," Tommy said. "She had a baby on her lap, and a toddler close."

"And there were two others, young, school age. First or

second grade, maybe."

"Well," Summer said, thinking, "we have dinner here, a dinner we can share. I'm sure we could also find some things to take over to make it feel like Christmas."

"I wish we can send our Christmas tree," Sophie said. "But I don't know how we'd do that, not if they don't have any electricity."

"You can always take our generator," Melvin said. "That would keep the house warm and provide electricity until we can get their power turned back on."

"That's a good idea, Granddad," Sam said. "I can load the generator into the truck."

"Did they have a fireplace?" Joe asked.

"It was the only source of heat," Tommy said. "But I didn't see a lot of wood, and what they had, looked pretty damp."

"We could take them a cord or two."

"We can put together something for their dinner and breakfast," Sophie said. "We have food, and our Christmas baking." She hesitated. "And the cinnamons rolls we made today for tomorrow morning."

For a moment no one said anything, and then Summer nodded, adding briskly, "If we're going to send the rolls, we should add one of the ham and cheese casseroles. That would make a very nice breakfast."

Cade wished MerriBee was here. She would love this. "I wish I had something to contribute—"

"You've just delivered twenty-four Christmas dinners," Sophie said, smiling at him. "I think you've contributed plenty. I also think you should head back to town. MerriBee will want to hear everything."

OVER A CHRISTMAS Eve dinner of grilled cheese sandwiches and tomato soup by the fire in the living room, Cade told MerriBee about the day, and the deliveries, and that last family who'd needed everything and how the Wyatts had rallied and came together to give that family warmth, food, and a Christmas. MerriBee listened in awe, touched and overwhelmed. The Wyatts had done a good thing, providing for the family in need, but Cade... he was amazing. He'd been downright heroic these past two days, having stepped up and delivered in a big way. She respected how he took charge, made quick decisions, demonstrating not just leadership, but his compassion for others.

She didn't know if he'd done it for himself, or for her, but either way, she was proud of him, and immensely grateful. His determination and effort meant everything to her. "You deserve a feast," she said, from her chair by the fireplace. "Not canned soup and a sandwich."

"I don't need anything," he answered, stretching out on the couch. "It was a great day. I feel good about everything."

He looked tired, but content, and she didn't think she'd ever be able to look at her couch without seeing his big frame there. He looked good there. He fit in her house. He fit in her life. If only he could see himself here.

"What is your plan for tomorrow?" she asked, having avoided the question all evening but anxious to know the answer.

"I'll probably be heading back to the Sundowner."

She suspected that would be the answer, but she had to ask. "I will miss you."

He turned his head, looked at her, expression somber. "You could come with me."

"I start work in a week."

"That's a week away."

"But then we just have to say all the goodbyes again, don't we?" She tried to smile, but failed. "I don't want to get kicked off the ranch again. That was mortifying the first time."

"I was hurt," he said, sitting up, feet planted on the floor. "And this time I'd have no illusions. I wouldn't let myself get carried away."

She hated how he said that... he wouldn't let himself get carried away... as if wanting her in his life was something too good to be true.

Her eyes met his and held. She loved him, so much. He was the one that was too good to be true. He was the one who could break what was left of her heart.

"I think I should stay here," she said unsteadily. "Start taking down Christmas and start thinking about getting back to work again."

HE WAS GONE the next morning, when she awoke. There was no fire in the living room, no coffee made in the kitchen. The house was dark, his room was empty, his truck was no longer in the driveway.

She hadn't expected him to leave so early, and she wished he'd woken her up before he left, but she also understood that neither of them was good with goodbyes. He'd done the practical thing, even if it made her chest hot and tender.

She made a small pot of coffee, and then carried her cup to the living room, and turned on the Christmas tree and sat with her coffee by the tree. The room was too quiet. She felt too alone. MerriBee rose and using her phone, put on some Christmas music, the sound coming through the wireless speakers.

That was better.

She sat back down, sipped her coffee, hummed along with a carol.

It was natural to feel sad. Cade lit up her world, made everything warm and bright and real. Of course it felt different now that he was gone. She was going to miss him. But soon she'd have work again. She'd be busy. She'd be fine.

A couple weeks ago her friend Taylor Sheenan had invited MerriBee to join her family for Christmas dinner, and

MerriBee had said no, but maybe she'd call Taylor and see if it was too late to join them. Getting out of the house would help. Being with others would help pass time.

At nine, she called her parents, wishing them a Merry Christmas, and then there was a family zoom where all her sisters and brother got on line to talk to each other. MerriBee did some baking after the zoom, wanting to take something to the Sheenan's Christmas dinner, even though Taylor said it wasn't necessary.

At four, she walked the short block to Troy and Taylor's. They lived on Bramble, in one of the older Victorian-era homes, their house painted a soft gray green, which looked stunning against the snow with the elegant greenery swagged across the front porch, and every window filled with a dark green wreath.

Dinner was wonderful, and crazy, and crowded, since this year Troy and Taylor were hosting Christmas for all their family. MerriBee only checked her phone a couple of times, just in case Cade called. He didn't, but Sophie Wyatt had texted, wishing her a Merry Christmas, and so had Ivy and Sam. There were messages from others, too, nurses she worked with at the hospital, as well as a voice mail from a doctor in Bozeman asking if she'd like to be his date for his hospital's annual New Year's Eve ball.

That last message caught her by surprise. She'd met the doctor a few months ago at a medical conference, and yes, they'd exchanged numbers, but she'd never expected to hear from him. She didn't even know what she'd done with his number.

It was almost nine by the time she walked back home. From a distance, her house looked like a gingerbread house with all the Christmas lights outlining the roof and windows. She was tired and ready for bed. She'd had a nice day but it would have been so much better if spent with Cade.

As she unplugged the Christmas tree in the living room she spied a present under the branches, half hidden by the velvet tree skirt.

There was no card or name tag attached, but she had a feeling she knew who it was from. Tearing off the paper, she lifted the lid from the box. Nestled in tissue paper was a vintage honeycomb honey jar, with a sweet single bee on the small ceramic lid. MerriBee lifted the lid and inside the jar with a note. *Merry Christmas for my Bee.*

Her eyes filled with tears. She didn't know when Cade had found time to buy it for her, but it was perfect.

CHAPTER TWELVE

CADE GOT A text late Christmas evening from Bee thanking him for her little honeypot. She'd added a heart emoji, and a little bee emoji.

He didn't know how to answer her text. Did he send a thumbs-up? Did he give it a heart? Did he initiate a conversation? In the end he simply answered, *Glad you like it.* And then he left it at that.

The next day he helped carry the luggage downstairs, and then load the different vehicles that would be ferrying the Jameses to the Sheridan airport. He wasn't unhappy that they were leaving, but the house would certainly be quiet. He hoped Dot was ready for the quiet as he himself was feeling very social.

For the next week, he worked with the ranch hands taking down Dot's Christmas tree, and putting away the decorations. Dot liked to leave her white outdoor lights up through January, claiming the month was so cold and dark she needed the bright white lights a little longer.

When he wasn't working, Cade returned to his cabin and shut the door and shut the world out. So far he'd done a good job blocking thoughts of MerriBee. He'd decided the best approach was to just pretend she hadn't ever existed, not because he had any desire to be ugly, but remembering her in any way created pain, reminding him of all that he'd never had, and of all that he still wanted.

Like love. And a family of his own. Holidays. Traditions. Hope. And maybe faith.

He admired MerriBee's convictions, wished he shared some of them, but maybe he could learn. He wasn't averse to growing.

On New Year's Eve, Dot always threw a little party for her staff at the house, serving the kind of food the guys liked—a huge prime rib, twice-baked potatoes, fluffy rolls, broccoli smothered in sharp cheddar. There were drinks, too, anything they wanted from her bar, but nearly all the guys stuck to beer, not wanting to embarrass themselves in front of their boss.

Cade wasn't drinking, and he didn't eat as much as he normally did, aware that this wasn't just the last day of the year, but also Bee's birthday. She turned thirty today. He wondered what she did for her birthday.

At nine o'clock, the ranch hands carried everything back to the kitchen and several tackled dishes while others broke down the card tables in the living room. Dinner in the living room with the ranch hands had been the tradition since Dot was a girl. It was the Warner way of saying thank you to the loyal staff, and also kicking off the new year with a cash bonus tucked in a small paper envelope. Cade always pulled the money together, but Dot handed it out to each of the men. Once every member of her staff had been thanked, Dot and Cade were the only two left.

"That was a wonderful dinner tonight," Cade said. "Emma is a genius in the kitchen."

"I'm glad she's here. She's always happy to sit with me when I get lonely."

It was the first time Cade had ever heard Dot mention loneliness. He sat down in a chair close to hers. "Do you get lonely often?"

"Everyone gets lonely. That's just part of life." She paused, reached into the side of the chair, and lifted out an envelope, slightly larger than the others she'd been giving the hands earlier. "I have something for you, Cade."

"It's not necessary."

"But you won't get it for a few years. I haven't shared this with anyone. You are the first, other than my attorney, to know. Cade, I'm leaving you the ranch. All of it. I can't think of anyone who would be a better steward for the Sundowner than you, you've not only been an honest, hard-working manager, you've been loyal to me. You've been my family. Obviously, I hope to be around for many years to come, but when I do go, I'll be able to rest, knowing that everything my grandfather worked for, my father worked for, and I worked for will be in good hands."

Cade struggled to absorb what he'd just heard. "I don't

know what to say."

"I'm sure it's a shock. I can't imagine you expected this."

"I didn't. Ever." He rose, paced the length of the living room, turning at the massive stone hearth. "Dot, I'm overwhelmed, and flattered, but I worry you're making this decision hastily. I'm worried that you're worn out from the Jameses' visit. I don't want to take something from others—"

"I never intended the ranch to go to them. I always thought it might end up with you, but I gave them a chance. I thought, they are family, they are nieces and nephews and second cousins, in the six years they've visited—seven this year—they've never shown any interest in learning about the ranch or managing it."

"You noticed."

"Of course, I did," she said indignantly. "I'm not a doddering old lady, letting them take advantage of me. I was giving them an opportunity to prove themselves. I was giving Alistair a chance to show me why his family should inherit the ranch. He never did. But you have. For sixteen years you have, even when you were in the army. You wrote me weekly, you phoned, you checked in, you handled problems as they arose. Even though you had a job elsewhere, you always managed to still take care of all of us here."

He didn't know what to say. He felt undeserving. "This is one of the great ranches in Wyoming, Dot."

"Exactly. I don't want to see it broken up, sold off, piece by piece, and that would happen in someone else's hands.

But not if it all goes to you. You understand the value of this place, and the history. It's also been your home since you were just an angry teenager and I looked into your eyes and dared you to be more. I challenged you to be the person you're supposed to be, and you did. You served our country. You've been a good steward of the land. You've taken care of me." Her eyes shone with unshed tears. "If I had a son, my hope is that he would have been half as loyal and loving as you."

Cade lowered his head, hiding his face, hiding the emotion. He'd never heard those words growing up. He'd never had praise, never felt loved. And then he'd taken a summer job here and it had saved him. Dot had saved him. He was overwhelmed by her acceptance and her faith in him. Even without shared DNA, she was the one who'd been there, and pushed him, and influenced him, and because of her, he was the man he was today. Not perfect, but able to love, to forgive, and, on a good day, forget.

"The deed to the land has already been put into your name," she added, holding out the envelope to him. "But the rest of it, the house, livestock, income will go to you upon my death." She shook the envelope at him. "Come take it. My arm is getting tired."

He crossed the room to take it, bending down to kiss her forehead as he did so. "Thank you, Dot."

"You're very welcome, Cade, and very well deserving."

"When do you think you'll tell Alistair?" he asked. "I'm

worried there will be blowback for you. He's not going to like it."

"Oh, I know. But I'm sure if I sent him one of my Remingtons or Bierstadts, perhaps a few of Daddy's gold coins, he'd be okay. Let's face it, whatever I give him he will just sell, creating a tidy nest egg, without all the responsibility of the lands, the cattle, the livestock. As well as my staff."

"You've seen him eyeing your artwork then?"

Her smile was impudent. "Hard not to. They weren't very stealthy. Especially when they'd look at a piece, then look it up online, and discuss the value should it go to auction. It happened more than once, and I was often just a room away. I might not have the best balance, but when my hearing aids are in and on, I have super hearing."

"Why are you telling me this now? Is it because of MerriBee? Are you trying to lift my spirits?"

"Did it work?"

"You've given me security, but even more importantly, you've made me feel as if I finally belong somewhere. It was good to find the Wyatts. It was good to know who my father was, but Wyoming is my home. The Sundowner is home. And you're my family."

Dot sat still, expression inscrutable. "Marietta is not that far of a drive, Cade. You could come on weekends to see me. We could do that zoom thing. We could stay in touch—"

"That's not enough. You should have family with you now. You should have me. I wasn't there for my mom, not when she needed me, and I'm not going to repeat those mistakes."

"I'm not dying. I expect to live another ten years."

"And I expect to be here for another ten years with you." His gaze met hers and held. "Let's be honest, what would I do in Marietta? I need to be outside, on land. I need a ranch to run. Cattle to chase down."

"What about the Wyatt ranch? I'm sure Melvin could put you to work there. He wants to get to know you better. He doesn't have very long, either."

Cade paced the room again, heart heavy, thoughts tangled. He'd never felt pulled like this before, had never felt as if he needed to be in two different places, for two very different, but important reasons. Montana represented the Wyatt family. Wyoming represented home. "I can drive to Paradise Valley on weekends now and then. I can spend time with my granddad, get to know those cousins of mine."

Dot's forehead creased. "And MerriBee? What about her?"

"I'm not going to do a long-distance relationship. I don't want that. My stepdad was on the road all the time and it wore my mom down. She hated it every time Jimmy left, hated being responsible for so much on her own."

"I have a feeling MerriBee isn't anything like your mom."

"No, she's not, but even then, I can't marry her and start a family if I'm not there. We're either all-in, or we're all out." He heard what he was saying and it made his chest burn. He hated letting Bee go, but it would be worse loving her, and leaving her, after just a few days together. Five days apart, two days together, five days apart... no. He couldn't do it. He wasn't good with goodbyes, wasn't good not being able to see, or be with, the person he loved.

"Have you two talked this through?" Dot asked.

He nodded. "It's why I'm here without her now. It didn't make sense to continue. We've broken things off."

"Completely?"

He nodded again.

"I'm sorry," Dot said, and she sounded genuinely disappointed. "And here I was thinking this gift of the ranch would help you to get started, provide security for your children. I would have waited for a better time—"

"It's okay. I think the timing is perfect. You've given me something to look forward to. I just wish I knew what to say other than you'll always be able to rely on me. I'm not going anywhere."

"Not even for love?"

Her words struck deep, straight into his heart. Her words made him question love. It made him question his feelings for MerriBee. It also made him question her feelings for him. He understood how important her work was to her, but she could be a nurse in Wyoming. There were hospitals and clinics thirty minutes away. Not to be crass, but people died in Wyoming, too. Not that he'd ever say that to her, but it hurt him that she needed to care for all these others, all those strangers, more than him.

He picked up his hat, nodded at Dot. "I'm going to go check on the boys. Thank you again, Dot. I'm grateful for everything. Happy New Year."

IT WAS ALMOST six when MerriBee snapped. She'd had a late birthday lunch with Sophie, Ivy, and Taylor before they all went home to get ready for their own New Year's Eve plans. MerriBee had declined the invitation to attend the Bozeman hospital ball, and she thought she'd been prepared for a quiet night in. Eat the rest of her birthday lunch salad, watch some movies, make some popcorn, try to stay awake until the ball in Times Square dropped, but as she looked into the pantry at the box of microwave popcorn, she remembered the last time she had popcorn. It was with Cade in his cabin. He'd popped the corn on his stove, the old-fashioned way, and then poured a half stick of butter all over it. It was greasy and salty and perfect.

She wanted that popcorn now. She wanted to sit next to Cade on his oversized manly leather couch and watch another dreadful action flick that he'd think was sweet and festive.

She missed the sound of his boots. She missed the way he made coffee in the morning, missed his cheerfulness as he took care of things around the house. Nothing was too much work for him. Nothing rattled him. Nothing was impossible. She liked that about him. Loved that about him.

Loved him.

John had been the most wonderful man. Even dying he'd been full of life. Maybe that was the part of hospice work she responded to. Dying people appreciated life. Dying people didn't have time to complain about little things. Dying people wanted to focus on all the good that was left, as in the end, only love remained.

But Cade wasn't dying and he appreciated life. He didn't complain about little things. He was grateful for the opportunities he'd been given.

Cade, who'd been raised with so little, had hopes and dreams... dreams that included her.

She had someone who wanted her, wanting a life with her, wanting babies with her, and she'd said no because she had *to work*.

To work. More like, run away. Hide.

Her need to stay in Marietta was based on fear. What if she gave up her job and ended up heartbroken? What if she gave up security to be alone?

And so she'd rejected him, deflected his love, afraid his love was temporary and would disappear. She'd been afraid she'd lose it—*him*—just the way she'd lost John.

She couldn't bear the idea of loving again, only to lose that love.

But wasn't that what had already happened? She had love

and she'd pushed it away. She'd chosen to be single over a life with Cade.

She'd chosen to be with the dying over a healthy, strong, gorgeous man who wanted to share a future with her. It didn't make sense. *She* didn't make sense. She was making decisions based on fear, not faith. What was the expression? Let go, let God? Because that was what she needed to do. Choosing Cade didn't mean her work was over. There was no reason she couldn't be a nurse in Wyoming. Maybe she wouldn't work at a hospital, maybe she'd focus more on being a death doula, or maybe she'd just find a place that needed a nurse. She could do just about anything, especially if she had Cade at her side.

MerriBee glanced at the clock. Six thirty. The ranch was a four-and-a-half hour drive. If she packed quickly and drove like the wind, she might be able to make it by midnight.

She drove like the wind, too, until the real wind came in, and lifted up the snow on the ground and blew it every-where, making it impossible to see. MerriBee passed Sheridan and knew she was getting closer, but the world beyond her windshield was so white, she wasn't always sure she was on the highway. There were no cars. There was no one else on the road to Story, the town closest to the ranch. She'd driven in harsh conditions before, but this was terrify-ing. She didn't know which lane to be in, didn't know what the road signs said, everything beyond her car covered by the blowing snow.

She cried earlier, so scared she didn't know if she should pull over, drive, turn around, keep going. But she couldn't cry and concentrate at the same time, so she dried her tears and kept driving, looking for the bumps on the side of the highway, as those at least reassured her that she was still going in the right direction.

As it neared midnight, she tried to call Cade but she wasn't sure if it was him, or her, but there didn't seem to be service, and because of the storm, her GPS was worthless. The exit for the Sundowner Ranch had to be coming up. She opened her window, craned her head out, looking for the hand-lettered sign that read SUNDOWNER RANCH ¼ MILE AHEAD. EXIT WARNER ROAD.

And there was the sign. She knew it was the Sundowner sign from the rustic wood and the blue lettering in one corner. One quarter of a mile more, and then she'd turn right onto Warner, and then it was just straight back all the way.

Thank goodness she had the highway to herself as she practically crawled that last quarter of a mile. And there it was, the big iron and wood arch, with the iron *W* indicating the entrance to the Sundowner Ranch. She breathed a massive sigh of relief as she turned up the road. Just a couple miles more. They were all uphill, up a steep mountain, but she had a good car, she had her snow tires, she'd be in four-wheel drive, there was no reason she couldn't do this.

She was doing it, too, until she hit ice and lost traction.

MerriBee panicked and hit the brakes, which made her slide worse. She took her foot off the brake immediately, but it was too late, she was sliding sideways, going backward, down the mountain road.

She couldn't get control. She was sliding too fast, and even though she tried to pump the brakes, nothing was happening. MerriBee crashed into a mound of snow on the side of the road, but at least she'd come to a stop and hadn't slid into a creek or a ravine.

MerriBee stepped from her car, surveyed the snow and the car's position. It was definitely stuck, but at least the car wasn't blocking the road.

She tried calling Cade again. But nothing. She looked at the time. Eleven forty-five. Almost midnight. She looked again at her car—she could stay in it and hope help came, or, she could walk up the rest of the mountain. The ranch buildings were maybe only another mile away.

Obviously a mile in snow and freezing temperatures wasn't a mile in sunny conditions, but she heard the song "Ain't No Mountain High Enough" in her head and decided to go for it. She'd always been athletic. She used to hike, rock climb, ski and skate, and she'd get to the ranch even if it took her all night.

IT WAS ALMOST midnight. Cade didn't feel like ringing in the new year with the ranch hands in the bunkhouse, especially as half of them were pretty drunk. He said his good nights and headed back to his cabin. As he walked to his place, he checked his phone. He'd texted MerriBee earlier, wishing her a happy birthday, and a happy New Year, but hadn't heard from her. He hoped she was out doing something fun. He hoped she had celebrated her thirtieth properly.

He was just about to open his front door when one of the young hands appeared. "The security cameras picked up activity on Warner Road. Someone is on the road, walking this way."

"Sure it's not a deer?"

"Mr. Hunt, I know what a deer looks like. It's a woman."

It couldn't be. There was no way. She wouldn't.

She would.

"Do you have keys for a snowmobile on you?"

The ranch hand patted his coat, and then his jean pocket, pulling it out from his front pocket. "The green one," he said, handing the key over.

"Thanks," Cade said, already running.

She was still over a mile from the cabin when Cade spotted her, trudging up the steep mountain road. Thankfully, the wind had died down and he could see her, doggedly marching through the freshly fallen snow with her cast, on a barely healed ankle.

She was crazy, and she was here, and Cade was never going to let her go, not without him. He pulled up next to her, turned the motor off. "What are you doing?" he said, dragging her into his arms.

"Coming to spend New Year's with you."

He kissed her. "Happy New Year," he said, lifting his head to cup her cold face between his hands. The tip of her nose was icy. Her lips were freezing. "You could have died out here."

"Not if I kept moving." She wrapped her arms around him, stealing his warmth. "How did you know I was here?"

"We have cameras that monitor the road. Where's your car?"

She gestured downhill. "Down there somewhere. I hit ice, lost control."

"You weren't hurt?"

"No. Just frustrated." She shivered. "Now that I've stopped moving, it is cold."

"Let's get you home then and into a warm shower." He sat back down on the snowmobile seat. "It's not a true double seat, so hold on tight," he said.

"Never letting you go," she said, sitting behind him.

He looked over his shoulder at her. "Promise?"

"Cross my heart."

THERE WAS SO much to talk about, but it could all wait until the morning. MerriBee was exhausted and happy to collapse

JANE PORTER

into bed. Cade claimed he'd worry about her all night if she weren't with him, so she put on one of his big soft flannel shirts and climbed into bed after her hot shower, and fell asleep in his arms.

When she woke up, it was morning, the winter sun flooding the bedroom with light. She knew Cade was an early bird, but this morning he was still in bed with her. He wasn't sleeping, though. He was facing her, watching her.

"Good morning." He smiled at her, a very lazy sexy smile. "How did you sleep?"

"Good. Great." His smile gave her butterflies, and she blushed. "This must be a first, for you, Cade Hunt sleeping in."

"Oh, I didn't sleep in. I was up at four thirty."

"But you didn't get to bed until almost one."

He shrugged. "I had things to do."

She couldn't stop just drinking him in. He was so big, so solid, so very alive. She'd been trying to protect herself from feeling all the feelings—love, desire, need—but her walls had all tumbled down and all she knew now was that she wanted forever with him. Whatever that looked like.

"Let me guess," she said. "You had to check on horses. Make coffee. Watch the sun rise? What do you have to do at four thirty in the morning?"

"Make a cake."

She sat up, tugging the flannel shirt down so it covered her thighs. "A cake."

He wouldn't stop smiling at her. "A thirtieth birthday cake, for my Bee."

"You know how to make a cake?"

"No, but that doesn't mean I couldn't try." He left the bed, disappeared into the hall, and returned a moment later with a black cast-iron skillet... cake. It was a yellow cake with a creamy chocolate frosting. It even had a handful of white candles in the middle.

"I didn't have any cake pans," he said, "but I found recipes for skillet cakes, and thought the best way to start the new year is with cake." Cade put the skillet on the bed, leaned over it and kissed her. "Happy birthday, Bee. So glad you're here."

"Me, too," she said, kissing him back, lightly raking her nails over his jaw, loving the rasp of his beard. "So glad you found me last night. It was cold. I was tired."

"I will always find you. I will always be there for you, through thick and thin."

"Richer or poorer."

"Speaking of which," he said. "I have something to tell you."

She shot him a quick, concerned look. "Bad news?"

"No, not necessarily. Just depends on what we want for our future. I know how much your life in Marietta means to you—"

"You mean more. So much more," she interrupted. "I don't even know why I was clinging to work, making that the reason why I couldn't move. I think I was afraid. I know I was afraid. Having loved John, and lost him, I was afraid that if I loved you fully, you'd disappear, and I couldn't stand it. Easier to push you away until I realized that I still lost you. So I decided to stop trying to play God, and instead act in faith, and here I am, hoping you still want me—"

"I do."

"And want that family with me."

"One hundred percent."

The corner of her lips lifted. "I love you."

"I love you, too," he answered. "I understand your fear, though. I have my own fears. But my gut says that we're stronger together than apart."

"We make a good team," she agreed. She climbed off the bed, picked up the skillet. "Now tell me your news in the kitchen. I'm dying for some coffee and cake."

EPILOGUE

Christmas a year later…

THE JAMESES DIDN'T return for Christmas the next year, which was just as well since it was a quiet holiday season. At least, it was quiet until MerriBee's water broke on Christmas Eve and Cade dashed MerriBee to the hospital in Sheridan. The baby, not due for two more weeks, came quickly, arriving just after seven o'clock on December twenty-fourth. It was a relatively easy first birth, no complications, and MerriBee and baby Grace Dorothy Hunt, weighing seven pounds seven ounces, returned to the Sundowner Ranch to meet Dot and settle in.

Cade was a bit shell-shocked that the baby came so early and so fast. MerriBee was just thankful Grace was healthy. She was also very bald. Not a speck of hair.

"Is that normal?" Cade asked, standing in front of the fireplace, holding his newborn daughter.

MerriBee was curled on the couch, so happy to be home. "Yes. Many babies start out bald. Especially redheads."

Cade's head lifted. He grinned. "Do you think she might be?"

"There's a strong possibility."

"Oh, I hope so."

"If she is, she'll be teased plenty. Red, freckles, ginger, carrot top—"

"I'll beat anyone up who calls her names."

MerriBee laughed. "You can't beat up kids, Cade."

"Well, they shouldn't call my daughter names."

"I have a feeling you won't need to fight her battles. With you as a dad, she'll be able to hold her own."

Cade crossed to the couch, kissed MerriBee, and then carefully handed her baby Grace. "With you as a mom, she'll be unstoppable."

MerriBee settled Grace into the crook of her arm. "She was determined to be here for Christmas, wasn't she?"

"Thank goodness you'd finished delivering all your Christmas baskets."

MerriBee laughed. "That's true. I had nothing else to do. I guess it was time to deliver her."

Cade sat down on the couch next to them, his arm extending along the back of the couch. "My beautiful girls. My very own family."

There was a knock at the door. Emma had promised to bring them dinner.

Cade rose to answer the door. A young woman stood

there in a puffy winter coat, a red knit cap on her head, long dark hair spilling down her back. "Cade Hunt?" she asked.

He nodded.

"I'm Briar Phillips. Your sister."

THE END

This Spring, it's Tommy Wyatt's story in MONTANA COWBOY PROMISE!

Cade's sister, Briar Phillips, will be returning in MONTANA COWBOY BRIDE in Spring 2023!

MERRIBEE'S CINNAMON STREUSEL BREAD

Cinnamon Streusel Topping

1/2 c flour

1/4 c brown sugar packed

1/2 tsp cinnamon

4 TBL butter cut into small pieces

Cinnamon Swirl

1/2 c granulated sugar

1 TBL cinnamon

Batter

2 c flour

1 tsp baking soda

1 tsp salt

1 large egg

3/4 c granulated sugar

1/2 c melted butter cooled

1/3 c sour cream

1/3 c buttermilk

1/2 c – 2/3 c whole milk

1 1/2 tsp vanilla

Directions:

Preheat oven to 350, spray a 9x5 loaf pan

1. Make the streusel topping and put in fridge
2. Max the cinnamon swirl and set aside.
3. For bread mix the dry ingredients in large bowl set aside
4. In medium bowl mix belted butter, sour cream, buttermilk, whole milk and vanilla.
5. Pour wet ingredients into dry, combine just until mixed. Don't overmix/
6. Pour half of batter into greased loaf pan. Add the cinnamon sugar, swirl in a figure S.
7. Carefully spread the rest of the batter over swirl.
8. Top batter with streusel.
9. Bake for 55-60 mins.
10. Remove from pan when cool. Enjoy!

THE WYATT BROTHERS OF MONTANA SERIES

Book 1: *Montana Cowboy Romance*

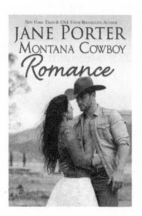

Book 2: *Montana Cowboy Christmas*

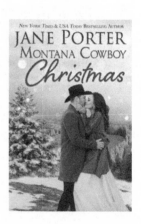

Book 3: *Montana Cowboy Daddy*

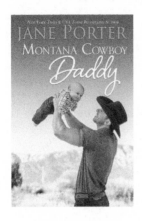

Book 4: *Montana Cowboy Miracle*

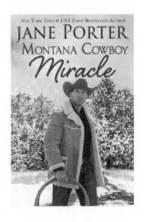

Book 5: *Montana Cowboy Promise*

Book 6: *Montana Cowboy Bride*

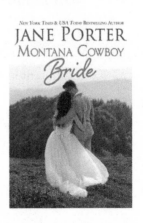

Available now at your favorite online retailer!

MORE BY JANE PORTER

Oh, Christmas Night

Love on Chance Avenue series

Book 1: *Take Me, Cowboy*
Winner of the RITA® Award for Best Romance Novella

Book 2: *Miracle on Chance Avenue*

Book 3: *Take a Chance on Me*

Book 4: *Not Christmas Without You*

The Taming of the Sheenans series

The Sheenans are six powerful wealthy brothers from Marietta, Montana. They are big, tough, rugged men, and as different as the Montana landscape.

Christmas at Copper Mountain
Book 1: Brock Sheenan's story

The Tycoon's Kiss
Book 2: Troy Sheenan's story

The Kidnapped Christmas Bride
Book 3: Trey Sheenan's story

The Taming of the Bachelor
Book 4: Dillion Sheenan's story

A Christmas Miracle for Daisy
Book 5: Cormac Sheenan's story

The Lost Sheenan's Bride
Book 6: Shane Sheenan's story

Available now at your favorite online retailer!

ABOUT THE AUTHOR

New York Times and USA Today bestselling author of 70 romances and fiction titles, **Jane Porter** has been a finalist for the prestigious RITA award six times and won in 2014 for Best Novella with her story, *Take Me, Cowboy*, from Tule Publishing. Today, Jane has over 13 million copies in print, including her wildly successful, *Flirting With Forty*, which was made into a Lifetime movie starring Heather Locklear, as well as *The Tycoon's Kiss* and *A Christmas Miracle for Daisy*, two Tule books which have been turned into holiday films for the GAC Family network. A mother of three sons, Jane holds an MA in Writing from the University of San Francisco and makes her home in sunny San Clemente, CA with her surfer husband and three dogs.

Thank you for reading

Montana Cowboy Miracle

If you enjoyed this book, you can find more from all our great authors at TulePublishing.com, or from your favorite online retailer.

TULE
PUBLISHING

Made in the USA
Las Vegas, NV
04 May 2024

89531856R00173